# THE DESERTER

# THE DESERTER

## Peter Bourne

MACMILLAN NEW WRITING

First published 2006 by Macmillan New Writing,
an imprint of Macmillan Publishers Ltd
Brunel Road, Basingstoke RG21 6XS
Associated companies throughout the world
www.macmillannewwriting.com

ISBN-13: 978–0230–00138–1 hardback
ISBN-10: 0230–00138–6 hardback
ISBN-13: 978–0230–00741–3 paperback
ISBN-10: 0230–00741–4 paperback

9 8 7 6 5 4 3 2 1

A CIP catalogue record for this book is available from
the British Library.

Typeset by Heronwood Press
Printed and bound in China

*To Caroline and Charlie and
my boys, Dominic and Matthew*

He who travels far will often see things
Far removed from what he believed the truth.
When he talks about it in the fields at home,
He is often accused of lying,
For the obdurate people will not believe.

— HERMANN HESSE

All you who pass, look and see: is any
sorrow like the sorrow that afflicts me?

— LAMENTATIONS 1:12

# Contents

# Afterwards

'I was going out for a walk in the sun, four or five days after the Nablus thing, and there he was in front of me, this guy. This small guy. Checked jacket, grey trousers, short mud-coloured hair, scuffed black shoes.'

Lev hadn't been back long. London seemed dull and cold after Jerusalem. Jo had chosen neutral ground, a little café near the British Museum.

'You seem to have a very clear picture of him.'

'I do, don't I?'

'Even down to his shoes.'

'Something about him must have alerted me. Alerted some sixth sense? Odd though that I should notice his shoes so clearly.'

'Especially since you pay such scant regard to your own. Yours are hardly ever shiny, always scuffed and dusty. Wasn't the state of your shoes an issue for your father?'

'Always. Anyway, there the guy was, standing on the path outside the front door to the apartment block. Not the door to Sarah's flat, you understand me? But the building's door, the one onto the street.'

'Is it so important?'

'Yes it is, Jo. Because of what happened later. He just stood there, halfway between the door and the gate, blocking the path. He said to me, "You're Lev Dubnow, aren't you?" I replied, "Yes, I'm Lev Dubnow. Why do you want to know?" He came up the path towards me. I was still standing on the step in front of the open door. He was looking up at me, defiantly, and he began yelling into my face, straight into my face: "But I don't understand. You're a Jew. You are, aren't you?" I was astonished. He repeated it again, "You're a Jew. You're Levi Dubnow's son. You're a Jew; you even look like a Jew. You were born into a good Jewish family. One of the best families! Yet you hate Jews." I shook my head at him, "I don't hate anybody—" He put his hand up, palm towards me, fingers parted like the spokes of a wheel. His hand was trembling so hard I could barely distinguish one finger from another. "Yes you do. Yes you do. I know you do. You hate Jews. You support the Arabs, the terrorists. You want us all killed." I had pulled myself together by this time. "Look, I don't have to listen to this." I went to close the door in his face but he put his foot against it. He clenched his hand into a fist and shook a single finger at me. His face was twisted, Jo, ugly, his eyes slits. "Yes you do, Lev Dubnow. I know all about you. You've betrayed your family, betrayed Israel – and betrayed your faith. You are a deserter. Deserter, do you hear? A deserter. You leave Israel, live for years outside. And now when you do finally crawl back, you don't come just to bury your father, just to mourn him, as you should, but you come to fight us, to fight with the Arabs, to join with them against us, us your people. The whole world is talking about you. You, Lev Dubnow, the great Nablus hero. Yet you're a Jew. I can see you're a Jew." He was screaming into my face, so close I could feel his saliva on my cheeks. I tried to be calm. I wasn't frightened exactly; he was so out of control and he still seemed to me such an insignificant little man. I told him to get his foot out of the door and when he didn't, I said to him, "Look, if you don't go now, I'm going to call the police; it's as simple as that." He laughed. "Call them then. See what they'll do. Nothing." I turned back into the hall and tried to slam the door. And it was then I felt a strange coldness in the middle of my back, and a pain so sharp it made me pitch forward. I fell against the door, hitting my forehead on something hard. Probably the door handle, I don't know. I must have twisted with the impact because the back of my head crashed against the floor tiles in the hall and everything went dark. When I woke up – it could only have been seconds later – I was surrounded by people telling me to lie still. There was blood in my mouth, Jo, there was blood; I could taste it. I felt like I was drowning.'

# 1. Overland from Amman

Lev got in from Beirut at around ten in the morning and took a cab straight to the King Hussein Bridge. Two and a half hours after landing at Amman's Queen Alia International Airport, he was walking under the huge circular twin portraits of the dead Hussein and his son Abdullah, the past and present kings of Jordan, into the Jordanian border post. As his cab had freewheeled out of gear down the steep curving road towards the parched white Jordan Valley, he had caught sight of a slate-grey stretch of lifeless water to his left. His map told him it was the Dead Sea. He tried to remember if he had ever been there as a child. He'd ask Sarah.

He was directed by a soldier at the border post gates across a dusty yard towards a freshly-painted single-storey terracotta-and-white building. It was one of a number dotted here and there around the fenced compound, built as the need arose rather than to any plan, it seemed to him. The light was very bright outside in the yard but not yet hot. The building he walked into though was dark and dismal and at first sight completely deserted. When his eyes grew accustomed to the sudden deep gloom, he saw that there was actually someone there, at the far end of a long hallway, looking at him through a glass screen. The man was in shirt-sleeves, although the warmth outside had yet to reach as far as the booth where he sat.

He smiled a welcome as Lev approached.

'Hi. Passport?'

'Oh yes, right. Thanks. I mean, eh, shukran.'

Lev handed over his passport, pushing it through a little half-circle gap at the bottom of the booth's glass screen.

'*Ufwan.*'

'Excuse me, do you speak English?'

'Yes.'

'Thank you. Thank you very much. That's kind. I've been told to ask you not to stamp my passport. Is that alright?' Everyone had told him that the last thing he needed was an Israeli stamp in his passport, and to avoid it at all costs.

The man grinned back at him.

'Oh yes, that's fine. We only stamp paper here.'

'Great, thanks, that's very kind.'

The light was so dim that he had difficulty finding the right note to pay the departure tax. It wasn't because of a lack of electricity; the smiling official was already registering his details on a computer.

'You don't like Jordan?'

'What?'

Lev was puzzled for a moment.

'You're leaving so soon.'

'Oh I see. I have no time, I'm afraid. I am going to Jerusalem to see my family. My father has just died.'

The man very slightly and very elegantly inclined his head down and to one side, gently closing his eyes for a moment and putting his right hand flat on his chest, his fingers splayed.

'I'll have a trip round on the way home, if I have time.'

'Petra is very beautiful.'

'So I've heard.'

Together with his passport, Lev was handed a little piece of paper, serrated down the middle, decorated with a coloured photograph of some Roman ruins and with the words 'Departure Tax Receipt' printed underneath on each half. On the back were two diamond shaped stamps in Arabic and in English, reading 'Departure from Jordan' with the date.

'Go down that corridor please. There is a bench. You will see. Have a good trip.' .

'I'm grateful. Thank you. That's very kind.'

'It's my job.'

The official looked curiously at him before turning back to his screen. Lev was aware that he was being exaggeratedly polite. It was probably because he was so nervous about the next few days and what might happen.

He walked down the corridor, past an unattended bag-scanner and back out into the sun. It was much hotter now. There was a bench across the yard, against the wall of one of the other buildings. Two men were sitting on it already. One was old, very smartly dressed in a slightly tight and old-fashioned brown pinstripe suit, and very English brogues which shone brilliantly in the sun. Surrounded by bags, and packages wrapped in brown paper and tied up with string, he was clearly not European. His complexion was dark and his skin deeply lined, with unhealthy-looking puffy folds of flesh under his eyes. He was dozing, his drooping bottom lip revealing tobacco-stained teeth in bad repair. Beside him was a much younger man, dressed in black trousers, black open-necked shirt and white trainers. There was a small red holdall on the ground between his feet. He was smoking. As

Lev sat down next to him he looked up and smiled.

'Hi.'

'Hello.'

They sat in silence for a few moments. The younger man was the first to speak.

'We seem to be the only internationals around here today.'

'Seems we are. Yes.'

'Getting hot, isn't it?'

'Very.'

Again they sat in silence.

'It'll take some getting used to.'

'What will?'

'The heat.'

'Certainly will.'

After another few moments of silence the younger man tried again, putting out his hand this time.

'My name's Jack.'

Lev would have been content to have continued sitting in silence, but shrugging his shoulders resignedly, he limply clasped the outstretched hand.

'Oh right. I'm Lev.'

'You're a Jew, right?'

'I am yes. Is it that obvious?'

'Yep. Once a Jew and all that. Like the Catholics.'

'Are Catholics so easy to recognise? It's not been my experience.'

Lev lit a cigarette of his own and looked across the compound at a scruffy little building he hadn't noticed before. Unlike the others, it was an earthy grey, and very badly neglected – almost derelict. 'DUTY FREE SHOP' was painted on a wooden board crookedly tacked up over its locked brown door.

Jack was short and stocky, very dark skinned. He had dark brown eyes, alert and quick. His black curly hair was worn longish to well below his collar.

'Well, I'm American.'

'I can tell by your accent.'

'American-Palestinian.'

'Palestinian?'

'Yep.'

They sat for a further few moments in silence.

'So what's your story?' Jack asked.

'What?'

'What's your story? How do you come to be sitting here next to me waiting to go to Israel?' He pointed at the deserted yard in front of them. 'It's pretty clear there aren't many other people making the trip.'

Lev felt disagreeable, peevish even. He couldn't help himself. He resented being found out so easily and so quickly, especially after his last few days of anonymity.

Lev had gone straight from the hospital to Heathrow after coming off-duty, without bothering to make a booking. He had taken the first available seat going vaguely towards the Middle East and had ended up in Istanbul. When he arrived he asked to be taken to the best hotel in town. After lapping up the overpriced luxury for two nights, he flew to Beirut. The next day he took a flight to Queen Alia.

It had been wonderfully exhilarating doing exactly what he wanted when he wanted, with no one around to remind him of how much everything was costing or arguing with him about what to do next. He lived – and had lived for most of his life – such a structured existence. As a hospital doctor for over twenty years he was invariably on call, living with the threat of his bleeper summoning him to some emergency. He had felt so liberated and carefree when he had locked the accursed thing away in his locker, walked out of the department and got on the tube to the airport.

'I think I'd rather hear yours, actually,' replied Lev.

'Right. Okay then. My parents were from Nablus,' said Jack. 'Do you know where that is?'

'Yes.'

'Right, of course you do. I was forgetting.'

'You're assuming a lot. Not every Jew is from Israel.'

'No, but you are, aren't you – or were, at least?'

'I was born in Jerusalem.' Lev didn't attempt to hide his irritability. 'Why don't you just get on with your story?'

Jack ignored the disagreeable tone.

'Right. Well, my dad left Nablus when I was four. He went to the US, worked for a few years as a porter in a vegetable market in New York, built up some capital and then went into business for himself in Boston. He did very well. He never went back.'

'Alone? Did he go alone?'

'No he took me with him.'

'What about your mother?'

'He left her behind. After a couple of years he divorced her and married Kathy, an American woman from New Mexico. She brought me up. They opened a deli in downtown Boston, specialising in Middle Eastern food, and we all lived in an apartment above it. Still do. Except I've been away at college in Michigan for the last three years. Just graduated. Civil Engineering. After this little trip is over, I'm going back to do my Masters in New York.'

'So you've come back to find your roots?'

'Pretty much. Yes.'

'It was a very unusual thing for your father to have done. How old are you now? Twenty-four, twenty-five?'

'Twenty-seven.'

'So he left your mother, your Palestinian mother I mean, something like twenty-three years ago. He certainly broke out of the mould, to have done a thing like that twenty-three years ago.'

'More than you think. My mum found out she was expecting just after we left.'

'And he still never went back?'

'Nope.'

'Bit of a rogue, your dad, then?'

'Rogue? Are you trying to be polite?'

'I expect he had his reasons at the time. There're usually two sides.'

'No two sides to it, Lev. He's not a bad man, my dad, but he was very selfish to have up and left like he did, without so much as a backward glance. That he's been a good father to me I can't deny, and he has always sent money back here for my mother and my brother. But he just wanted out, and to him then that was all-important, so he just left. He wanted what he calls now a real life. Even in those days it was pretty wretched for Palestinians – although it seems it is much worse now. At least they could get work in Israel then. He finally made up his mind to leave just after the Camp David Accords. It had become a bit easier to emigrate. My mum didn't want to go, so he just left her behind. I was only four. It was pretty cruel to us both. Don't you think?'

'A tough decision certainly. Why did he take you with him?'

'For my education.'

'So this is your first time back since you left?'

'Yep.'

'And you've got a twenty-two-year-old brother you've never met?'

'I have.'

'And your mother?'

'She died a couple of years ago. Dad didn't tell me until months after he'd heard. Otherwise I'd have been over before now. I'd have come over then, if he had told me.'

'Why do you think he didn't?'

'Wanted nothing to do with his old life? Guilt? Would have felt obliged to come with me? We had a furious row when I found out. He said he didn't think it would be so important to me, seeing as Kathy had been such a good mother and seeing as I had been so young when we left.'

'And your brother, what's happened to him?'

'Waseem, that's his name, looks after my uncle's land north of Nablus, near Tulkarem. My uncle's an old man and not very well. Olives, almonds and a few sheep and goats, from what I can gather. I'm about to find out, aren't I? As long as the Israelis let me in, that is.'

'Why shouldn't they? You may have been a Palestinian once but you're an American now, aren't you?'

'Once a Palestinian ...'

'Surely it wouldn't be in Israel's interests to make it difficult for visiting Americans? A bit counterproductive, I'd have thought.'

'I'm still a Palestinian in their eyes, despite my passport. They call us a 'problem', or haven't you heard?'

'Of course I have. My father spent most of his youth pushing you lot around. I'm not sure how things stand now though. I've been gone a long time, Jack. I've tried hard not to think much about 'the situation' these last few years. Sometimes Israel has seemed very far away. From the little I've bothered to read, both sides seem to me to be as bad as each other.'

Jack grunted disapprovingly and continued.

'Perhaps I should have tried to get an entry visa before I left. Some people said I should. But I somehow thought I'd have a better chance with border guards than with the embassy in Washington. They'll have less chance to think about it, won't they? And I'm told this particular border is the easiest to pass through because of agreements with Jordan. I've come a very long way to be turned back.'

'We'll find out soon enough.'

'That's for sure.'

They sat silently again for a few minutes.

'So what about you?'

'You're very persistent, Jack.'

'Hell Lev, what else is there to do while we're waiting for something to happen? People say you can sit here for hours just waiting. But if it's private, if it's too personal, that's OK.'

'No, it's not particularly private, it's just that I've done my best over the years to put all the Jewish stuff and the conflict on the backburner. Much like your father seems to have done. It was all part of an old life. And then you picked me straightaway and I felt I was right back in it. I didn't pick you for anything other than a Yank. How come you can get away with it and I can't?'

'You've never really been part of a minority have you?

Not a repressed one anyway. Makes you aware of these things, always on the lookout. For self-protection, more than anything else.'

'Is that it?'

'I think so. You're probably right about my dad. He might deny it if you confronted him with it but I think he has tried quite hard to forget his origins too. He certainly doesn't much like being 'picked', as you call it.'

'Is he ashamed of being an Arab?'

'Probably.'

'It's clear you're not.'

'Are you ashamed of being a Jew?'

'I don't lie about it if that's what you mean, but sometimes, in a muddled sort of way, I wish I wasn't.'

'They are your people, Lev.'

'It carries a lot of baggage, being Jewish. Baggage that I don't want and that sometimes I'd quite like to be relieved of.'

'And yet now you're going back.'

'I am.'

'Why?'

'Because ...'

'Yes?'

Jack grinned. Lev grinned back despite himself.

'OK, you win. Firstly, I'm a doctor – that's what I do. I work in a hospital in central London but I was born and brought up in West Jerusalem. My mother died when I was in my late teens and I have a brother and a younger sister, neither of whom I have seen for a very long time. My sister does write once or twice a year, so I haven't been completely cut off. I met an English girl called Joanna. She was visiting

Jerusalem, as 'a concerned tourist finding out about Israel'
– her words, not mine. We met in a little cafe just inside Jaffa
Gate. It worked between us from the start. After a few weeks
we started talking about getting married. My family didn't
much like the idea – they didn't much like her either, if
truth be told. She was a bit outspoken for their taste. And of
course she wasn't Jewish. That didn't help matters, as you
can imagine. So I upped and left Israel with her and, after a
brief spell in South Africa, settled in London. As a doctor it
wasn't hard for me to get work. Later on I took British citizenship. An Israeli passport isn't very useful if you want to
see something of the world, and Joanna and I liked travel-
ling. In the end we never actually did get married and now
we've split up.'

Lev sighed and bit on his upper lip.

'These things happen.'

'And then last week my father died.'

'I'm sorry.'

'Thanks. These things happen as you say. So what I'm
doing today is going back to see my brother and sister and
to attend a memorial function that my brother's organised.
A gathering of Dad's old military cronies, in other words.'

'So this is your first trip back too, since all that?'

'It is. I'm not relishing it as you can imagine. Still, it has
to be done, I suppose.'

'It's right that you should pay your respects, Lev. Your dif-
ferences with your father in the past don't affect that.'

'It'll be nice to see my sister. But my brother Udi? That's
another thing altogether. I haven't heard a word from him
since I left. Surprising, I sometimes think.'

'And you? Have you tried to make contact with him?'

'No.' Lev reddened a little. 'No I haven't. Should have, I suppose.'

'Takes two.'

'I rang Joanna before I left England, to tell her I wouldn't be around and that I was coming over here. Her reaction was just as surprising. She's always been forthright but she was really quite tough when I told her I was going back to Israel. Harsher than she normally is, than I expected her to be. Some people find Jo sharp, even confrontational. I never have. She has great compassion but she is not easily sentimental. People misunderstand her. She's very bright that's all. She sees things clearly where others see only complexity.'

Lev looked embarrassed.

'Sorry, I'm being boring.'

'No you're not. You were saying you rang her. So what did she say?'

'She said, "I don't know why you want to go back there just to celebrate that unpleasant old man's life. You'll only have to meet that awful brother of yours. It'll only distress you. What are you hoping to gain from it?"'

'And what did you say?'

'That I thought I might achieve some sort of a closure, a binding of the wounds.'

'Reasonable enough.'

'You'd think so, but she scoffed at me.'

'She did?'

'Yes, she said, "Claptrap! More like some sort of a re-opening." I wonder whether it is going to turn out that she was right.'

'That you'll be opening up old wounds?'

'Yes.'

'Depends on how much guilt is still hanging around and how you all handle it. Guilt is so unproductive, don't you think?'

'You mean, what's done's done so move on and forget it.'

'Forgetting is pretty unproductive too. There's no problem with remembering; remembering helps with making sure whatever it was happened doesn't happen again. There's no purpose in feeling guilty though, just as there's no point in holding a grudge, looking for revenge or harbouring bitterness. They just damage the present, undermine the future and usually make moving on, as you put it, impossible.'

He looked up.

'Here we are, this'll be for us I should think.'

An empty coach was reversing onto the large white rectangle painted on the asphalt in front of them. The driver got down and threw open the vehicle's side-lockers. They both helped the old man with his luggage. He said nothing, just smiled gently. Lev wanted to take his own bags inside but the driver insisted that he stow them away in the lockers. They both eventually followed the old man up the steps of the coach and found themselves seats next to each other. The upholstery was newish but very dusty. Jack tapped the back pocket of his jeans.

'What are you looking for?'

'My passport. Have you got yours on you? I'm told you're going to need it before you see your bags again. And a pen too, while you're at it. Don't forget your departure slips either. Someone's bound to want to see those. They are your only evidence that you've actually left Jordan.'

Lev got out of the coach, quickly retrieved one of his

bags and took a pen and his passport out of the zip-up pocket in the side. The slips were safe in his passport. He packed his bag away again and got back on the coach.

'It's really hot out there now.' He gazed out of the window. 'Where do you think this coach is going to take us?'

'Across the bridge I suppose.'

'Is it that far?'

'I wouldn't have thought so.'

'So why can't we just walk across?'

'Containment? Security? I don't expect they want anyone drifting about.'

From various bits of shade a dozen or more people suddenly materialised. They were instructed by the driver to put their bags in the lockers before they got on the coach. It didn't seem to matter to him how small a bag was, they all had to be stowed underneath. He was quite adamant about it. Slamming the lockers shut, he got on to the coach and closed the door firmly behind him, then sat down and lit a cigarette.

Lev whispered, 'What are we waiting for?'

'Search me.'

From behind a building on the far side of the compound another coach appeared, identical to the one they were on but crammed with passengers. Its side-lockers were so full they couldn't be securely shut.

'Who are they then?'

'They'll be Palestinians I should think. They'll be either Palestinians who now live in Jordan, going on a visit to see relatives, or Palestinians with Israeli citizenship who have been to Jordan or elsewhere abroad and are going home. What you can be pretty sure of is that they are not

Palestinians who live on the West Bank or in Gaza – the Israelis rarely allow them to go anywhere.'

'It's crammed. Why haven't we seen any of them before? There's so many of them, we could hardly have missed them.'

'There'll be another entrance for them somewhere. They will have been dealt with separately, in a different building.'

'I didn't see another entrance.'

'It's probably somewhere round the back.'

'Is that why almost everyone on here looks European?'

'Yep.'

'But what about the old man who was dozing on the bench next to us? Wasn't he a Palestinian?'

'He can't be. I suspect he's a Jordanian – I mean a *Jordanian* Jordanian, rather than a *Palestinian* Jordanian. He might be an Egyptian, I suppose. He certainly won't be Syrian or Lebanese. I don't know about Turkish but he doesn't look Turkish does he?'

'He's not wearing a fez you mean and sporting a shaggy moustache?'

'Take it easy. I didn't mean anything.'

'Sorry. No I know you didn't. A legacy from Joanna, I'm afraid. Bless her.'

'Who? Oh, you mean the woman you ran away to England with.'

'Yes. She could get very exercised by people being stereotyped by their appearance.' Lev sat deep into his seat. 'I experienced something like this a long time ago. In Cape Town actually.'

'In South Africa?'

'Yes. Jo was determined to see for herself what it was really like for the Blacks. She called it "witnessing". We thought that perhaps South Africa might be a bit of a challenge so we took a little holiday, to psyche ourselves up before going. We fancied somewhere exotic and went to India. Did the Taj Mahal, Delhi, Rajasthan, all of that. Eventually we jumped a boat from Bombay, as they used to call it then. People often "jumped boats" in those days. You'd fly now, wouldn't you, but then we "jumped a boat". A steamer – there's another word you don't hear anymore. Jo was pregnant by this time. In fact she was pregnant even before we had left Israel, although we didn't know it. She became determined to give birth in South Africa. She wanted to give our child "a fully developed conscience" about apartheid, or some such non-sense. Although it didn't seem nonsense at the time.'

Lev laughed thoughtfully inside himself.

'What a lot of burdens the poor kid would have been expected to carry. I wonder if he would have been up to it. Such a great deal would have been expected of him if he had lived. But he didn't. He bloody died.'

'I'm sorry. Was he ill?'

'Two weeks premature. Wouldn't have been a problem in England, he would have had a better-than-evens chance if we had gone straight to England. All that nonsense about "a fully developed conscience". I should have insisted. I didn't though did I? I went along with her. Her conviction was new to me; I loved her for it. Still do, despite what happened then, and what's happened to us since. Incompetent ruddy doctor, I'm afraid. I can't be completely certain, because they wouldn't let me in the delivery room ... *We do things differently here, Dr Dubnow. We know what we are doing.*

*She's in good hands.* But what I do know is that look of panic on doctors' faces when things are going wrong and they don't know what to do. I've seen it too often. And it was on that doctor's face when he came out to tell me our baby was dead.

Lev sat for a moment, drumming his fingers on his knee. 'Are you alright?'

Lev looked at Jack's concerned expression and smiled.

'Yes, I'm fine. Got over it a long time ago.'

'Happens quite frequently in Palestine. More frequently now than before, from what I hear.'

'However frequently it may occur, I can't believe it doesn't still leave a scar.' Lev sniffed and rubbed his nose. 'Anyway before all that happened, we were on the boat to Cape Town from Bombay. During the trip we shared a table with an Indian family from Port Elizabeth, a mum and dad and three children. Originally from Gujurat I think. They had been back there to see the grandparents and were going home. We all got on very well. I can remember us saying to them that we should all meet up, once we had got ourselves settled. When we docked at Cape Town we couldn't see them anywhere while we were disembarking. Much as I did today, Jo and I just marched down the gangway and into the main arrivals hall. As we were filling out our immigration forms I looked across and saw them. They were on the other side of a wrought iron partition; I couldn't understand what they were doing there and how they had even got there in the first place. Jo and I hadn't seen the alternative entrance for non-whites, you see. Hadn't looked for it and hadn't seen it. The confidence of our colour had led us, without hesitation, into this clean, well-lit area, and their consciousness of their colour and what it meant in South Africa had forced them to look carefully around and find the separate entrance set aside for them – "somewhere round the back", probably – which had led them to the dimly-lit, cramped arrivals hall where they, like us, were completing their forms. I felt so ashamed.'

'Don't beat yourself up about it, Lev. The taxi driver who brought you today knew where you had to be dropped and dropped you there. So of course you unhesitatingly went in. What else would you do? Likewise the driver who brings Palestinians knows they have to be dropped somewhere else – and they, just as unhesitatingly, go through that gate. As for South Africa, you just didn't appreciate how total and immediate the separation of the races was, whereas your Indian family did. On both occasions, when you found out, you were troubled by it. It would be much worse if you shrugged and lamely accepted it as most people do.'

'That's a very positive take. Doesn't make me feel any better, but thanks anyway.'

The Palestinian coach was driving out of the compound.

'At least they're on their way.'

Three nuns bustled out of the gloomy depths of the departure building. They wore grey shirts, cardigans, skirts to just below their knees and long white linen cloths on their heads, pushed unfussily behind their shoulders. They came across to the foreigners' coach and rapped on the door to be let on. The driver got out of his seat, opened the coach door and obsequiously helped them one by one up the steps. They left their baggage on the ground for him to stow away, which he did as soon as he had settled them in their seats. They brought on little knapsacks and he didn't object. In fact he put them, one by one, very carefully up on to the empty baggage racks above their heads.

'So they're the reason we've been waiting here for so long,' said Lev.

A uniformed official got on and checked everyone's passports, while another man, in a sweater and jeans, collected fares. When they had both got off, the driver started up the coach and drove it out of the compound, following the same route that the Palestinian bus had taken ten minutes before. He drove along a straight road for about 300 metres, bare flattened sand on either side, to a bar gate where a Jordanian soldier checked everyone's passports again and tore off one half of the departure tax receipt. The bar then creakily rose and they drove along a narrow, slowly winding road, past a couple of canvas-shaded gun emplacements, until suddenly, after about a kilometre, they drove out onto a concrete bridge.

Jack tensed.

'What's the matter?'

'I've got such a bad feeling about all this.'

'Let's just enjoy the moment. Hymns have been written about crossing this river. They will or they won't let you in, but there's not a lot you can do about that at this precise moment, is there? So just relax and enjoy yourself.'

'I'll try Ben Gurion if they won't let me in here, and to hell with their entry stamps.'

At the point where the squat concrete bridge crossed the river, the Jordan Valley was not much more than two miles across. It was flat and high-sided, as if a carpenter had precisely sliced it from between the Jordan Mountains in the east and the Judean Hills in the west. Snaking through the valley's centre was a ribbon of dusty green vegetation which almost completely concealed the narrow river itself – bleached dry fronds, tall green grasses, and stocky palm trees, all struggling for life under the high hard sun. Crosscurrents turbulently rolled across the river's surface as it rushed under the bridge.

The day was clear, bright and sharply hot, despite how early in the year it was. In the coach it was suffocatingly close. Lev felt as if the sun had chosen him specifically to shine its rays upon. His skin prickled as if it was being attacked with pins. If it had been after April, his back would have been running with sweat and his shirt saturated.

The mountains he was leaving behind appeared stony and dry but, as he had noticed that morning, they were in fact fertile and productive, heavily terraced with grey-green olive trees. The hills he could see in front of him though were arid, harshly yellow-ochre in the midday sun. Low and conical, with grooves radiating from their summits, they interlocked impenetrably, an impassive barrier defying assault. The valley floor around him, though essentially flat, had been ravaged by centuries of desert flash-floods into an intricate tangle of deep dry trenches between jagged mounds of hard white sand. Dotted across this remarkable landscape were a handful of ineffectual-looking gun emplacements, looking increasingly toy-like as they grew smaller with distance, their long slender turrets pointing into the bright blue sky.

Their coach stopped suddenly.

'Here we go Lev. The first checkpoint.'

'Not quite.'

The first checkpoint was actually still thirty or forty metres further on. They had cleared the bridge but another barrier with a single horizontal bar had stopped them. The

Palestinian coach was parked at the checkpoint ahead, its passengers huddled together under a freestanding shelter with a corrugated iron roof. A boy in dark khaki fatigues was inspecting the underside of the coach with a round mirror on the end of an adjustable pole. As Lev and Jack sat waiting for the bar to be raised, another coach crossed the bridge. It looked brand new and had only a few passengers on it. Edging its way past them it drove round the checkpoint where the Palestinian coach was parked, and disappeared behind one of the low jagged mounds of white sand. This particular mound had a short stick planted in the top of it with the blue and white flag of Israel flying from it.

'What's that all about?' said Lev. 'VIPs?'

'I've no idea.'

A woman with a wonderfully strong face and powerful penetrating eyes leant forward between the seats.

'Israeli bus with Israeli passengers.'

Her English pronunciation was precise but heavily accented.

'Don't they get checked?'

She paused, considering her reply carefully.

'They must at some stage, I suppose. I do this trip every month and I've seen lots of Israeli buses going through like that. I've never seen one stopped. I must introduce myself. My name is Elizabeth Mann, I am a resident pastor in Amman. I come to Jerusalem every month for a meeting.'

Lev squeezed his hand between the seats to shake hers.

'My name is Lev; this nervous chap here beside me is Jack.'

While they were speaking, the Palestinian coach had begun to move off and, as it did, the bar in front of their vehicle was raised and they drove down the hill to take its place. Their driver turned off the engine, and the young boy in fatigues who had been inspecting the underside of the Palestinian coach got in and collected all their passports. He took them to a man with a shaven head, wearing completely opaque sunglasses. He was dressed in a white t-shirt and jeans, cowboy boots and a grey bulletproof jacket. He was leaning against a sand-bagged shelter covered in sand-coloured netting. It looked like a sentry box; an unattended rifle, trained on their coach, nestled between two sandbags.

'Who do you think he is?' asked Jack.

'Some sort of security guard I suppose. I don't know. Elizabeth?'

'Security. Border Security I think. Or National Security. They look different every time. Sometimes they wear suits.'

'Bit hot for suits today.'

'Don't these guys ever wear uniforms?'

'Not that I've seen.'

'Are they always men?'

'Mostly. Lots of the ordinary soldiers are women of course.'

'My God, he is really built isn't he? He looks pretty uncompromising.'

'They generally are very uncompromising, I'm afraid,' said Elizabeth. 'Whether they are in cowboy boots or smart suits doesn't seem to matter.'

They watched him leaf through their passports. When he had finished he put them in a tidy pile on the ledge and beckoned everyone to get off the coach, indicating with a wave of his hand that they should all go and stand on the asphalted space under the shelter. Bordering the space were what looked to Lev like half a dozen English park benches. No one sat down. Jack was smoking nervously. Meanwhile the boy in fatigues had opened the coach lockers and, after inspecting their bags, began looking underneath the coach with his mirror.

One by one the muscular guard called them towards him by name. As each approached he checked the photograph in the passport against the face in front of him. After twenty minutes or so they were all back on the coach.

'I'm through the first one, at least.'

'Jack, don't worry, you'll be fine.'

'We'll see.'

They were off again but were soon halted for a third time by a set of traffic lights on red. The traffic lights were bolted to one of two steel watchtowers on either side of the road. The watchtowers were clad in the same sand-coloured camouflage netting. Artillery pieces pointed out from what looked like little wooden cabins perched high up on top of them. The cabins had blank, long horizontal slits in their walls for windows, and Lev had no doubt they were being spied on from up there. Wandering around between the watchtowers were two girls and a boy, again in khaki fatigues. These three, though, were carrying guns.

'Elizabeth, are those kids soldiers?'

'They are.'

'But they're so young. They should be in school or at university or something.'

'There is compulsory military service here at eighteen, for all except a very few.'

'But those kids look much less than eighteen. Perhaps I'm just getting old.'

'They are much too young for the unpleasant work they have to do, that's for sure.'

The traffic lights turned green and the coach drove on. After another few hundred metres there came into view a long single-storey building with a green glass porch which projected out over an area of asphalt full of baggage and people. Parked at the kerb, still crammed, was the Palestinian coach with its door closed and its engine turned off. Their coach parked in front of it. The driver instructed them all to get out, collect their own baggage and join the crowd already waiting. Walking around the front of the coach having retrieved his bags, Lev stopped and stared, surprised at what was now in front of him.

'Look Jack, look over there.'

He was pointing, away from what he had taken to be the border terminal, towards a neat oval lawn, uniformly green and perfectly mown, with budding jacaranda saplings in perfectly circular beds at regular intervals around its border.

'That would do credit to a bowling club in Godalming.'

'Godalming?'

'Oh it doesn't matter, just some little town south of London. It must take hours of work and gallons of water to keep it in that condition in this climate. Think of the effort! Why would anyone bother?'

'No effort spared to impress! They make the desert green around here. Haven't you heard? There you have an example of what can be done. Before your very eyes! I think Israel believes it's making a significant statement to every visitor who comes through here.'

'It might be if it was the first thing visitors saw when they came across the border, but it's not is it? We've been checked and grunted at by a thug in opaque shades, watched over by children dressed as soldiers, and spied on from the top of net-shrouded watchtowers. It looks to me defiantly eccentric, sinister.'

'Sinister? It's only grass Lev.'

'It's more than that. We are in occupied territory aren't we? But most people, people outside the Middle East anyway, don't realise that, they think the Palestinians are in control here but actually the Israelis are. There might as well be a sign on one of the trees saying "We're here to stay". It reminds me of the village greens British colonials used to plant in Indian towns during the Raj. Jo and I saw a few of them when we were there. Occasionally there was even an English country church as well. It used to be explained away by saying that they were planted out of nostalgia for the old country. Joanna used to say that was only half the story and that really they were statements of British authority and permanence.'

'Does every opinion you have stem from your Joanna?'

'She thought about all these things in much larger terms than most people seem to.'

They were now standing at the back of a crowd of twenty or thirty people. Most of them appeared to be Palestinian. There were lots of child soldiers hanging around looking bored. Some were wearing bulletproof jackets. Others had taken theirs off because of the heat and had hung them carelessly over the line of blue and white metal barriers which prevented people from wandering off. The crowd was bunched tight.

'Who does he think he is, strutting about?' Jack was pointing now. 'Look at him. He's almost identical to the one at the first checkpoint, except he's carrying a weapon.'

'A guy like him, armed but in normal everyday clothes, feels more threatening to me because he's *not* in uniform. If someone's wearing a uniform it feels as if he may, at least, be accountable, that he will be under orders. That chap looks as if he could do whatever he liked to us and get away with it.'

At the back of the porch, there were five glass booths. Three were empty. In each of the other two sat young women in grey open-neck shirts and unbuttoned dark blue epaulettes. A porter was collecting each person's baggage and passport. He put the baggage on a trolley, flung the passport on top, and pushed it all towards one of the booths where he handed the passport over to the woman inside. She then counted the separate pieces of baggage and printed out two bar-coded labels for each item. The porter stuck one on the back of the passport and the other on a piece of baggage, then put the baggage on a conveyor belt and brought the passport back to its owner.

'That all looks pretty straightforward.'

'Awfully slow though, Lev. This could take hours. Some people here have got five or six pieces of luggage.'

'Well we'll just have to be patient then. Want a cigarette?'

Lev handed Jack the packet.

Elizabeth had skirted round the crowd and had already managed to have her single small bag taken by one of the porters. Jack caught sight of her going through the double doors ahead of them. He waved and she called over, 'See you inside.'

Eventually the porter came for Lev's luggage. When he got his passport back he hung around waiting for Jack. A slight breeze had sprung up. It felt like a hairdryer and gave no relief at all, blowing hot dust in everyone's faces, making eyes smart and lips taste salty. When Jack was done he sauntered across.

'The Palestinian coach is still parked there you know.'

'Waiting for us all to clear, I suppose.'

'Why don't they just let the passengers out to stretch their legs, get some air? It must be really hot in there.'

'Stifling I should think.'

They pushed at the double doors and entered a large, high-ceilinged space, like a school assembly hall. Dividing the room were three long counters and two walk-through body scanners with long queues. There were benches against two of the walls. A few people were sitting on them, including the old man from their coach. Jack and Lev joined separate queues.

Before walking through the scanner, Lev had to give his passport to an official, a middle-aged man in blue shirt and trousers, with a lanyard over his right shoulder. He flicked through the pages, stopping to look at some of the old visa stamps. Finally he read Lev's personal details on the inside back cover.

'You are from?'

'England.'

'Jerusalem?'

'No England. UK. I was born in Jerusalem but I am a British citizen now.'

'Where are you going?'

'To Jerusalem.'

'Ah! Why?'

'My father died last week.'

'I'm sorry.'

He inclined his head down and to one side and put his hand flat on his chest, his fingers splayed. His eyes did not close though. Rather they remained fixed on Lev, sharp and watchful.

'Thanks. That's kind.'

'Your job?'

'I am a doctor.'

'You work for?'

'The NHS.'

'The N …H …S?'

'Yes, I work for the National Health Service in England.'

'Is that an organisation that helps Palestinians?'

'I beg your pardon?'

'We have a problem here with Palestinians. You don't know we have this problem?'

'Yes of course I do but the NHS has nothing to do with the Palestinians.'

'And it does? What does it do, this Service?'

'You don't know what the National Health Service is?'

'I think it supports the Palestinians against Israel.'

'No. It provides healthcare to people in Britain. It is a free service. It's famous.'

'Famous? I've not heard of it.'

'You haven't? I'm surprised. Anyway, it has nothing to do with the Palestinians. It is for British people.'

'For British people?'

'Yes.'

'And you are British ?'

'Yes. You are holding a British passport in your hands.'

'But you are from Jerusalem and now you are going to Jerusalem.'

'Yes my father has just died. I told you.'

'OK. Go through. Put all your belongings in here. Have a nice day.'

He indicated a small plastic tray beside the scanner and tossed Lev's passport on to it.

'What? Watch, wallet … all that sort of thing?'

'Everything. Everything. Cigarettes, money, lighter. Everything.'

Lev emptied his pockets into the tray and walked through the scanner. There was a high-pitched whistle.

'Back. Take off your belt please.'

'Oh right.'

'Lev took off his belt and walked through. Again the scanner screamed.'

'Back. Shoes.'

'Shoes?'

'Shoes.'

'OK.'

His belt now gone, Lev's trousers were beginning to slip down over his hips. He had to crouch down first on one knee and then on the other to pick at his laces. He felt a fool and was beginning to get flustered. The official just stood there and waited, watching him impassively. Eventually Lev put his shoes on the tray, but because there was quite a pile now, one of them slipped off onto the tile floor. The official still did nothing. Lev had to get on his hands and knees and drop his head almost to the floor to peer underneath the counter. When he finally found his shoe and got back on his feet, he balanced it precariously on the pile and walked through again with his hands in his pockets to keep his trousers up. The scanner screamed.

'Back. Jacket.'

Lev took it off, rearranged the tray so that nothing would fall off this time, folded his jacket, gently laid it on top and walked through the scanner. It was silent. He turned back to collect his things and was stopped by a girl in the same uniform as the middle-aged official, but minus the lanyard. The epaulettes on her shirt were dangling and unbuttoned like the women in the booths outside.

'Excuse me.'

'Yes?'

She held up a black handheld detector that looked like a TV remote control.

'Oh I see.'

She ran it up and down his chest and back, and the inside of both legs. When she had finished she smiled politely.

'Thank you.'

'You're not taking any chances.'

She smiled. 'I'm sorry?'

'Nothing. It doesn't matter. Can I collect my things now?'

'Go ahead. Have a nice day.'

Lev's irritability returned. He pointed at her dangling epaulettes with a smirk.

'Making some sort of fashion statement?'

'I'm sorry?'

He shrugged. 'Nothing. Have a nice day yourself.'

While he was collecting his things and rethreading his belt, he looked around for Jack. He had been stopped and was sitting on the benches at the far end of the hall. He glanced up and saw Lev looking at him; Lev spread his hands as if to say 'Why? What's going on?' Jack just shrugged and looked back at his feet but then looked up again, smiled wanly and waved Lev to go on and not wait for him.

Lev called to the man with the lanyard.

'Why has my friend been stopped?'

'Stopped? Who?'

'My friend over there.'

'Passport.'

'What do you mean passport? He's an American.'

'Passport. You go through there now.'

He pointed towards another set of double doors.

'But—'

'You want to go through or not?'

'Yes, but—'

'Good. Have a nice day.'

He turned back to what he was doing.

Lev looked back at Jack. He was staring at the ground so Lev slipped his jacket back on and walked towards the next set of double doors. Beyond them he found himself in another great space. He saw Elizabeth and went over to her.

'Do you know they've stopped Jack?'

'I'm not surprised.'

'He's an American.'

'He's a Palestinian, Lev, as far as the Israelis are concerned. Like you're a Jew.'

'How do you know? Jack knew immediately too.'

'It was clear from the moment I first saw you. The security people have recognised you as a Jew too, you can be sure.'

'Ah, but they can see from my passport that I was born in Jerusalem.'

'Lev, they knew you were a Jew immediately. They didn't need to look at your passport. Discrimination is very highly developed here, very subtle. It is the same wherever people are frightened of each other, where the next person you meet on the street might want to hurt you. More so, probably, than it ever had to be in the old South Africa. You were there weren't you? Didn't I hear you telling Jack? I think the situation here more closely resembles your Northern Ireland. In South Africa it would have been relatively simple: the enemy was black and the good guys were white – or the other way round of course, if you were black. Here though, everyone looks much the same, more or less. And even when they don't, some of them can still turn out to be Jews, the Ethiopians for instance. Because of that, successful discrimination is really quite difficult. As a result there is a highly developed subliminal consciousness of who and what people are. You don't have to be here long to develop it. I include myself in that. You may resist, but when you live for any time at all in a culture where discrimination between one group and another is so rife, the ability to instantly discriminate develops very quickly. It cuts both ways of course. Arabs need to be able to identify Jews too. They have to protect themselves just as much. They would probably say more so. From the Israelis' point of view, every Arab is an enemy or a potential assailant. So an unerring identification of everyone they meet is essential to their survival. They mustn't ever be caught out if they want to stay safe.'

'Hi you guys. I'm through.'

'So what happened?' said Lev, relieved to see Jack.

'One look at my passport and I was sent to sit on the bench and told to stay until I was called. It was only when there was no place left to sit that they finally called me.'

'Weren't you given the third degree?'

'Nope. Just searched and scanned and sent through here.'

'Why was I given such an interrogation then?'

'I've no idea.'

'He was just being inquisitive,' said Elizabeth. 'It is not

his job. He's there to make sure you are not carrying anything nasty, that's all.'

'So what do we all do now?'

'I have a special passport, so I don't have to see anyone
in particular. You two, though, have to get entry visas. I
hope you've got a good story, Lev. If you haven't they'll put
a stamp in your passport for sure.'

'I've been told all about that. I've thought one up, don't
worry.'

'Don't make it too complicated; you may have to remember it at a later date. OK then. Good luck to the both of you.
Especially to you Jack.'

They found the forms, filled them in and went up to the
desk. There were three women inside, behind glass, talking
and laughing amongst themselves. All their epaulettes dangling of course. One of them looked up as they approached
but turned her eyes away, continuing to talk to her friends.
They waited. After a few minutes Lev cleared his throat
audibly.

'I beg your pardon. Is this where we get our entry visas?'

The woman looked up again but this time put out her
hand.

'Passports.'

They handed them over.

'Forms.'

'In the passports.'

She gave Jack's passport and form to one of her colleagues and began leafing through Lev's.

'Excuse me.' He cleared his throat again. She looked up
at him. 'I've been told to ask you not to stamp my passport.'

'Why? Why don't you want your passport stamped?'

He lied. 'I have to go back to the Lebanon. I'm told the Lebanese authorities won't let—'

'Why?'

'Why what?'

'Why are you going to the Lebanon? Do you know anyone there?'

'No. I am going to meet my girlfriend.'

'Is she Lebanese?'

'No, English.'

'You live in Beirut?'

'No.'

'Does she?'

'No.'

'Do you know anyone in Beirut?'

'I've already told you. No.'

'Why are you both going to Beirut then? The Lebanon is hostile to Israel.'

'My girlfriend is flying to Beirut from England to meet me there for a holiday. Afterwards we are going back to England together.'

'You have your ticket?'

'What ticket?'

'Your ticket back to England.'

'No. She's bringing it with her when she comes.'

'When is she coming?'

'In about a month.'

'She's coming to Israel first?'

'No she's flying straight to Beirut.'

'Why? She knows someone in Beirut?'

'No.'

'What is her name?'

'Robin. Robin James.'

Lev was caught off guard by the question and was startled by the name he chose. After his separation from Jo he'd had a knee-jerk fling with Robin James, an old friend of theirs from South Africa.

'Why are you coming to Israel?'

'My father has just died. I'm visiting my family.'

'I'm sorry.'

Her right hand went half-heartedly to her chest.

'Thanks.'

'Your father was an Israeli?'

'Yes, he was.'

'Name?'

'What, my father's?'

'Yes.'

'Levi Dubnow.'

'Do you know anyone in Israel?'

'My sister.'

'Name?'

'Sarah. Sarah Dubnow.'

'Address?'

'It's on the visa form. In Rehavia. I will be staying with her.'

'Anyone else?'

'Anyone else what? At my sister's. My brother-in-law, I imagine.'

'No. Do you know anyone else in Israel?'

'My brother.'

'Address?'

'I'm afraid I don't know it offhand. My address book is in my bags and you've got those.'

'Name?'

'My name is Levi Dubnow. Like my father. It's on my passport.'

'No, your brother. What's his name?'

'Udi. Udi Dubnow.'

'Anyone else? Do you know anyone else in Israel?'

'Not really. I've been away a long time. I've lost touch with friends over the years.'

'Where are you going to visit?'

'Jerusalem.'

'Only Jerusalem?'

'As far as I know, yes.'

'Are you going to the Territories?'

'No.'

'Do you know any Palestinians?'

'No.'

'How long are you going to stay?'

'No more than three weeks.'

'You were born in Jerusalem?'

'I was, yes.'

'When did you leave?'

'About twenty or so years ago.'

'Why?'

'I went to live in London.'

'Why?'

'I met an English woman and went to London to be with her.'

'This English woman, she is the girlfriend you are meeting in the Lebanon?'

'I don't see it's any of your business.'

She ignored him.

'Why don't you have an Israeli passport?'

'Because I became a British national.'

'Why?'

Lev was getting impatient.

'You must know why. I'm sorry but you know very well how inconvenient it can be to have an Israeli passport. For goodness sake, if there was even one of your entry visa stamps in my passport I couldn't get into the Lebanon to meet my girl-friend, could I? It makes it harder to get a job, too.'

'What is your job?'

'I'm a doctor.'

'Israel needs doctors. Just one moment.'

She got up abruptly and walked across to a door two or three metres away. As the door shut behind her, he caught sight of a balding, overweight man in plain clothes sitting at a terminal gazing keenly though thick-lensed glasses at a computer screen.

Meanwhile Jack had undergone a similar interrogation. The woman who had questioned him had gone through the same door.

'Did yours take notes?' he asked. 'Mine didn't.'

'Neither did mine.'

'I had the impression she was asking questions almost for the sake of it.'

'What do you think they are doing in there?' Lev pointed at the closed door.

'Reporting to someone higher?'

'I hate to think how garbled her version of what I said is going to be!'

'Mine didn't seem to think that going to visit my brother was much of a reason for wanting to enter Israel. She asked me if I knew any terrorists. As if I'd tell her! She didn't much like the idea I was going to Nablus either. She said it was a base for terrorism.'

'Well, is it?'

'A major source of resistance against the occupation? No doubt of it.'

'Well then ...'

'So that makes everyone in Nablus a terrorist does it?'

'Obviously not everyone.'

'What sort of person would you call a terrorist then Lev? Think about it for just one moment. Are legitimate protesters, people who demonstrate, terrorists? In many countries they frequently get shot down as if they were. Are pilots in F16s who bomb peoples' homes terrorists? Are their officers who give the orders? Are the kids who throw stones at tanks cruising down the street outside their houses? 'Terrorist' is a much-abused word.'

'But what about suicide bombers?'

'If your husband and children had just been killed by a rocket hitting your car while they were waiting for you to come out of a shop, how would you respond? With sticks and stones? Sticks and stones have been tried and all that happens is that those throwing them are mown down by tanks or helicopter gun-ships – much like the grass on your Godalming lawns, and with just as much efficiency and precision.'

'You are sounding like an apologist.'

'I am? Is that bad?'

'If someone were to consider you to be excusing the inexcusable, calling you an "apologist" would be a way of dismissing you as not worth listening to, and your opinions as irrelevant nonsense.'

'Then that would be very unjust, wouldn't it? I'm not attempting to excuse or justify suicide as a weapon of war. What I'm doing is defending those who choose to fight with their lives by explaining their motives and the perfectly coherent arguments that underpin them."

'It's complicated, Jack'

'No it's not, it's quite straightforward. I'm surprised your Joanna hasn't enlightened you. Beware of those who call problems "complicated": they will be either incompetent or very dangerous. Either way they are untrustworthy.'

He paused and looked around.

'You may think that the Arabs have made a hash of negotiations over the years, that they've been intransigent – and in many cases I would agree with you. But the issue itself is still really quite simple. The Israelis are an occupying power. They are occupying someone else's land. They even call it "the Territories". That's not complicated, Lev. How is it any different from the French Resistance in the thirties and forties?'

Lev looked at Jack. He genuinely liked him, even after such a short acquaintance. Lev's friends all lived in London, and most of the closest ones were women. There were, though, three or four men he loved – Joanna used to call them his 'soulmates'. What they all had in common was that they didn't compete man against man, as most men instinctively seemed to. Jack was the same. If their relationship extended beyond today, he was a likely candidate for Lev's select little band.

'You've obviously thought a great deal about all this.'

'Of course, I'm a Palestinian. And it's not easy, believe me.'

'What's not easy?'

'To think.'

'I don't follow.'

'In the States the current polemic is so anti-Arab, so anti-Palestinian, that it's very difficult to think clearly, to keep a balance. I have some knowledge – second-hand, most of it, but knowledge nonetheless, and much more than the average American.' Jack lit a cigarette. 'So-called suicide bombers are always portrayed in the West as terrorists and extremists.'

'*Militants and insurgents.*'

'Those too. The West and Israel are deluding themselves. By demonizing and dehumanizing "suicide bombers", they fail to recognise them for what they really are.'

'And that is?'

'People, Lev, ordinary everyday people, and what is more, people who are desperate and people who are beaten. When suicide bombers start appearing in a conflict, the conflict is already won – and the suicide bombers are not on the winning side. It seems to me that neither the West nor Israel, if it comes to that, is anywhere near understanding that. To call them cowardly is plainly absurd. I'd have thought that targeting your enemy from 5,000 feet and pressing a button as if you were playing a computer game is infinitely more cowardly than determinedly giving up your life.'

The ash on the end of Jack's cigarette was now longer than what was left of the cigarette itself, and when he finally took a drag it disintegrated and fell on to his trousers. He brushed it off distractedly.

'This probably isn't the time and the place to be having such an earnest conversation.'

'Here is as good a place as any,' said Lev.

'There's lot of CCTV around. I would be astonished if

there weren't a few microphones strategically placed here and there. Call me paranoid, but it wouldn't be beyond the realms of possibility that they've been listening to everything we've been saying and are deciding whether or not to give us entry visas on that basis. If that's the case then I've had it, haven't I?"

'You'll be alright. This has to be the last hurdle, surely?'

'You've got a lot to learn, Lev.' He glanced up. 'Here we go. Here's your woman at least. Fingers crossed.' He hesitated. 'Look, hold on a minute Lev. I really don't think I'm going to get through – no, don't say anything, just listen.'

He gave Lev a piece of tightly folded paper.

'This is my brother's address and my address in Boston as well as my email address. Will you go and see Waseem? If I'm there, fine, and we'll all have a great time. If I'm not, tell Waseem I tried. And perhaps you can let me know how he is, if he needs anything. You know the sort of thing. Anyway please take it. Here put it in your pocket. You will go, won't you? I know it's a lot to ask.'

'Don't worry, of course I will. I'll be pleased to.'

'Are you sure?'

'Yes I'm sure.'

'Thanks. Look, your woman's ready for you. As long as she gives you the green light, you go through. Don't wait too long for me on the other side. Go on. Off you go. Good luck. With the family and everything.'

Lev went up to the desk. Before he reached it, she had already stamped the bottom half of his visa application form and was stamping her copy.

'Have you stamped my passport?'

'No. You asked me not to.'

'Thanks. How long have I got?'

'You have three months. Please go through there. Have a nice day. Enjoy Israel.'

She was pointing at a narrow gangway between the desks. Lev looked back for Jack but couldn't see him.

He was now in another great space. There were three rows of seats directly in front of him, all occupied. His entry visa was checked immediately by a young woman behind a desk at the end of the gangway. She directed him towards another desk in front of a glass screen. At this desk there was yet another woman. She was sitting behind a monitor and asked Lev for his passport. She turned it over, passed the barcoded labels across a sensor and gave it back to him.

'Please wait. Your bags are not cleared yet.'

'Why not?'

'They are being searched. You'll have to wait. Please sit down over there.'

The seats were all full so he had no choice but to lean against the wall. He waited for what seemed ages although it was probably no more than twenty minutes. The woman behind the monitor called names from time to time and either sent people out past the glass screen directly behind her, or through a small door to her left. Other people came through that he recognised – the old man in the pinstripe suit gave Lev a weary wave – but Jack still didn't appear.

Finally Lev heard his name called.

'That's fine. Your bags have been cleared.'

The woman indicated where he had to go by flicking her thumb over her shoulder. Before going through, Lev looked back to check whether Jack had finally come through. He hadn't.

Lev's luggage was in a heap with dozens of other bags, suitcases and parcels, dumped like so much rubbish. He picked them up and walked towards the double doors at the far end of the baggage hall. It was five o'clock in the afternoon and outside the sun was low in the sky but still warm. The light was clear, vibrant and wonderfully bright.

The next time he met Jack was in New York a year later. Lev was there on holiday; Jack was doing his Masters. He had been turned back at Allenby, and again two days later at Ben Gurion. He was not given a reason on either occasion.

* * *

There was a line of taxis in front of Lev as he walked out of the baggage hall. He went up to the first one.

'Jerusalem. Rehavia.'

'Fifty dollars.'

'But it's less than an hour's drive! In Jordan—'

'This isn't Jordan. Fifty dollars, boss. The price is fifty dollars.'

'OK.'

He threw his bags on to the back seat but got in beside the driver. Before they had even left the car park he had fallen sound asleep.

Lev had a slight headache when he woke up. He felt very thirsty.

'Tired, boss? My name is Sami.'

'Sami. Right.'

'My card, boss. You need a cab. Call me.'

'Your card. Right. I'll keep it. Thanks.'

Lev looked around.

'Where are we?'

'Not far.'

'But I don't recognise this. Where are we?'

'You know Jerusalem?'

'Once, very well. I expect it has changed a great deal. I've been away more than twenty years.'

'Long time, boss.'

'Yes.'

Lev didn't feel inclined to talk. He looked out of the window with an overly concentrated gaze and Sami seemed to take the hint. He would be at his sister's quite soon, and he would have to do lots of talking – and of course he would have to meet his brother. He felt apprehensive suddenly.

The taxi stopped.

'Where are we? This isn't Rehavia.'

Sami smiled a feeble smile and shrugged.

'No permit for Jerusalem, boss.'

'What?'

'No permit, boss.'

'You mean you are not allowed to go into Jerusalem?'

'No boss. Here only.'

'Why?'

'No permit. Can't get one, boss.'

'Why?'

'Palestinian, boss. My house is in Jericho.'

'You're not an Arab Israeli, is that it?'

'That's it.' He laughed. 'That's it!'

'You should have told me. Why didn't you tell me?'

Sami shrugged again.

'No business.'

He pointed through his windscreen at a mound of concrete blocks which was entirely blocking the street.

'Over. You go over, boss. Taxi to Rehavia on the other side.'

'Oh great, and I suppose you still want the fifty dollars?'

Lev thought about how much he had spent in Istanbul and Beirut, on hotels and taxis, on room service at two o'clock in the morning. He paid up. Sami was visibly pleased. He jumped out of the cab and got hold of Lev's bags.

'I help you, boss.'

Out of his taxi, Sami was surprisingly big. A good head taller than Lev. His monotonous 'boss' routine somehow diminished him physically. Given his size, it was clearly intentional. Lev however felt very safe beside him as they approached the barrier along the ill-lit street. There were a lot of people here swathed tight against the approaching night and the chill that was coming with it. They flitted silently around them like wraiths. Lev would have felt quite intimidated had he been alone.

The barrier was easily three metres high. There was a narrow gap between a couple of concrete blocks about two metres above the ground. Heaps of rubble and an old office chair had been piled up, making a rudimentary set of steps.

'Wait a minute Sami. Sami wait." He gently put his hand on Sami's arm, who stopped and stood beside Lev. 'I need to watch this for a moment.'

People, lots of people, were climbing through both ways. Old men with walking sticks, women in long skirts, some with children. The smaller children were lifted up hand-to-hand over the top to other hands. Sometimes bags and bundles were just tossed over; others were lifted carefully hand-to-hand. Two young men heaved themselves over and walked off without even interrupting their conversation.

Sami was aware that Lev was surprised at what he was looking at.

'Now you see how we live, boss.'

'What's this place called, Sami?'

'Abou Dis, boss.'

'I had no idea.'

'Been away a long time.'

'A very long time, it seems.'

A woman with an unhealthy-looking distended belly could hardly squeeze through the gap. Lev looked down at his watch.

'I must go now, Sami. Will you help me? I'm not used to all this.'

Sami was silent.

'Will you help me?'

'Sure, boss.'

Lev waited in line. Sami handed Lev's bags to an elderly man who was just about to climb down on the other side. The old man lifted them over and passed them down to someone on the other side.

Lev turned to Sami. 'Thanks very much for all your help.'

'Call me, boss, when you want a cab.'

'Back to the border you mean? I will, I promise.'

'Bye, boss.'

The rubble stairway was more unstable than it looked and the chair rocked a little as Lev put his full weight on it. He was putting his hand up to steady himself and to haul himself up to a little platform fashioned out of broken bricks, when he lost his footing. He cut the palm of his hand quite nastily as he grabbed at a piece of rope that was hanging there. He felt someone's hand under his sliding foot, which gave him just the purchase he needed to clamber up on to the platform. Even then he still had to twist his body round a projecting metal loop before he could get his knee on it. Eventually he managed to get his foot up and then stand up straight. Looking down he saw that a flat concrete slab had been leant against the barrier making a ramp so that it was relatively easy to get down to the ground on the other side. His bags were waiting for him, lined up neatly side by side.

As he bent down to gather them up, two tall young women passed him with books and files in their arms. The first one darted up the ramp and nipped up onto the little broken brick platform. The second one then handed all their things up to her, which she passed down to other hands on the other side before disappearing. The second woman though wasn't quite so agile. Just as her foot landed on the platform the heel on the shoe of her other foot caught in the hem of her jilbeb and ripped it. She looked down for a moment regretfully and then with a heave pulled herself through and disappeared after her friend.

It was almost dark now. The sky underlit by the setting sun was a brilliant deep blue.

Lev was called at in Arabic. He looked back. He was being asked to help. He was handed down a succession of black plastic bags full of boxes of coffee cups and saucers and finally a large white carrier bag full to bursting point with gentlemen's black umbrellas. Their owner, a very striking looking middle-aged man in a very high quality jalabia, ran down the ramp with little rapid steps, picked them up and thanked Lev with a quick nod before stuffing them through the rear door of a brand new Mercedes that had been waiting for him. The car roared off up the road, with a slight scream of wheel spin.

Lev's hand felt sore now that he was holding his bag. He found that the palm was covered in blood. He used his handkerchief to wipe off as much blood as he could, then folded it into a pad and put it over the cut, holding the handle of his bag tight to keep it in place.

An empty taxi was parked on the other side of the road. There was no driver. He looked around. After a few minutes a thin, pale-looking man emerged from under the ragged awning of an abandoned petrol station. A huge boulder of rough concrete had been put where cars would have parked to fill up, presumably to make sure that business couldn't easily resume.

'Is this yours?' Lev pointed at the cab.

The man nodded. He looked exhausted and not at all enthusiastic by the prospect of having to go to work.

'Great. How much to Rehavia? Will you take me to Rehavia?'

'Fifty shekels.'

He was too tired to argue and it seemed vaguely fair.

'Fine. OK.'

The driver was already wearily picking up the bags to put them in the boot.

Lev got into the back and slumped across the seats.

They got underway, shudderingly at first – there seemed to be some problem with the handbrake. They drove along a winding street round a sweeping U-bend and then began to climb steeply. At the top of the hill was a small flat roundabout which the driver disregarded completely, driving straight over it. He then slipped the vehicle out of gear and drifted downhill. Before them suddenly was the Old City. Huge walls, the golden dome on Temple Mount, and the chaos of pitched roofs, flat roofs, towers, steeples, terraces and balconies. It appeared to Lev as though it was all just about to slide downhill into the valley.

The traffic on Derech Ha'ofel meant that they made very slow progress. By the time they reached the area where Lev's sister lived, it was completely dark. The street lighting was not much better here than it had been at Abou Dis. He had difficulty recognizing anything familiar although he had known this area very well as a student.

'I think it's this street here. Yes here. The place I want is on the right.'

The taxi stopped suddenly.

'Why are we stopping? It's somewhere down there on the right.'

'Police. We must wait.'

Lev peered through the smeared windscreen. There appeared to be no street lighting at all down Sarah's road. Across the entrance was a string of blue and white metal barriers and beyond them a group of boy soldiers and some police, all in blue bulletproof jackets and carrying automatic weapons with short stubby barrels. The whole place had been cleared and there were only a couple of parked cars left in the darkness of the otherwise empty street.

'Bomb scare. Bomb scare.'

The driver clearly wanted to leave. His face had become suddenly pale.

'Don't you like the look of this? I can understand that. Just let me get my bags out of your boot.'

Before either of them could move there was a tap on the

driver's window. It was one of the policemen. He asked for their IDs. Seeing that Lev only had a passport he took it away and showed it to his colleague. They both looked carefully through it. The policeman hadn't returned the driver's ID and he was becoming increasingly agitated.

'Look I'd better pay you and as soon as you get your card back you can leave. I'll be alright from here.'

It was clear the driver couldn't care less whether Lev was going to be alright or not, he just wanted to get away. After a further few moments the policeman wandered back and returned their documents to them. As Lev climbed out of the cab, the policeman turned to him.

'Welcome home Dr Dubnow. Your father was a fine man. My condolences on your sad bereavement.'

'Thank you, that's very kind, but how did you know my father?'

'Oh, he was well known around here, sir, very well known, always walking the streets as he did during his last few days. Such a brave man, your father. A good man. It is fine for you to go now, sir. The incident is over. We can never be too careful though can we, sir? We must be always vigilant, the situation as it is. Your sister's block is down there on the right. 16a. Goodnight, Dr Dubnow.'

'Goodnight officer. Goodnight. Thanks for your help.'

'Nothing, Dr Dubnow. It's nothing, sir, nothing at all.'

Sarah lived in a squarish four-storey building. On the top floor there were balconies on each corner. Smart once, the building was now rather neglected. It was of little architectural merit or grace: slabs of rough, cream-coloured Jerusalem stone, metal-framed windows. A raised concrete path led to the block's front door, a small well-tended garden on either side. When they were children, Sarah had a little patch of garden all to herself, which she took great trouble and care with. Lev wondered whether she looked after these plots for her neighbours. He rang 16a.

The loudspeaker crackled and there was a cough.

'Who is it?'

'It's me Sarah. It's Lev.'

'Lev?'

'Yes.'

'Oh my goodness! Is it really you?'

## 2. Family Matters

Sarah hesitated briefly on the doorstep, just gazing at her brother, her eyes clouded by held-back tears. Then, in a rush, she ran at him and hugged him long and tight, imprisoning his arms in her embrace.

'I thought I'd lost you. I thought I'd never see you again. You've been gone so long. I couldn't really believe it when you said you were coming back. I've missed you so much.'

Lev waited for a few moments, giving her some time before gently releasing himself and holding her by the shoulders at arms' length. The wound on his hand was still bleeding and he left some blood on her shirt. She didn't notice. Her voice had deepened considerably since he had last seen her and she had put on weight, but otherwise it was as if he had never been away: there was the same look on her face as there had been on the day he had finally left, after the last confrontation.

They had all been in the large public room on the first floor of the family house, the room where those guests who were not close friends or relatives were received and where, as children, Lev and his siblings were only allowed to enter on special occasions. In it were all the beautiful things, the heirlooms – the precious Meissen figurines his mother had collected, antique furniture from Grandfather's house in

Minsk. It had three heavily-curtained ceiling-to-floor windows, each of which opened out onto a separate balcony,
where smokers congregated on nights when the Dubnows
entertained. On that most awful of days, Lev had nervously
taken refuge on one of those balconies before his father
and brother arrived. There was no great view – just their
small garden protected from the narrow street by a high
wall, and the house opposite, identical to theirs.

It had all been Udi and his father that day. Lev had main-
tained a dogged calm, while Sarah stood in agitated silence.

'Don't you realise what you're doing? How you are splitting the family? I am only grateful that your mother isn't
here to see it. She would be grief-stricken. Have I been such
a bad father? I've done my best with her gone. Our ideas
and principles – aren't they yours now, Lev? Do you not
share them with us any longer?

'Has he ever really shared them, Dad? They have never
ever been good enough for Lev Dubnow. Well have they,
Lev? Nothing's ever good enough for Lev Dubnow!'

'Have you always despised us so much? Is it really all to
do with that woman? Be rid of her Lev. Where's your loyalty
to us – your family, your faith, to the nation that's nurtured
you? Is your loyalty to her stronger? And your mother's
memory? Do you feel no duty to live the life she wanted for
you, that she planned and hoped for you? And what about
my grandchildren? Are you really going to give this all up?
Is it so easy to desert us all, Lev? And for what? For what,
exactly?

'A promiscuous bit of European skirt Dad, that's what!
He's drowning in the sea of his own lust.'

'For so little. For so very little. This Joanna of yours – take a step back, Lev, look at her for once, for what she really is.'

'She's no more than a self-opinionated, ridiculous little tart, if you ask me.'

'She is someone, Lev – and you will find this out for yourself in time, if you persist with her – who has no respect for religious belief of any kind. She doesn't understand the love we feel for our country, she has no conception of how important the soil we stand on is to us. How could she? I don't blame her for that. Her history is not ours. Did her grandmother die at Treblinka? Did her father lie hidden in the bowels of a freighter for a month only to be shot at and wounded by British troops as he finally set foot on this precious land? No. Her history is not ours, Lev. She cannot understand.'

'She actually told our father he was blind to the damage we have done here. Damage? What damage? Tell me that!'

'We have made this country, Lev, rescued it from nothing. It was a wasted land before we came. She said our behaviour towards the Arabs was cruel and barbaric. She says nothing of their barbarity towards us!'

'How dare she speak to him like that? Why do you not reprimand her? Is your father of so little importance to you now?'

'Can't you see, Lev, if you go ahead with this you'll make yourself an outcast? An outcast from everything you know and, despite what you think now, everything you love. Why are you so silent?'

'Obduracy Dad. Obduracy. He's determined. You'll not shift him. Give up, Dad. Give up on him.'

'Lev, it is if as you've gone from us already.'

Silent throughout, Sarah had stood with her back against

the cabinet where the Meissen was kept, her arms across her chest as if she was cuddling herself, biting fretfully at her bottom lip. On her face had been the same expression of moist-eyed vulnerability Lev saw now. Catching sight of that expression on that final day, he had felt his resolve wavering. He steeled himself again when his father delivered his final onslaught, his eyes dulled with bleak fury.

'I forbid you, Lev Dubnow, to marry that woman. If you do, I don't want to see you in this house again. I'll forbid Sarah and Udi ever to see you. I'll make sure you are cut off, root and branch. If you leave us Lev, desert Israel for this woman, you'll be no son of mine.'

Sarah released herself and rubbed her eyes briefly with her knuckles. Without giving him a chance to say anything, she grabbed his bags and walked into a dark hallway, illuminated by a single night light on a little table against the wall. She started to climb up some stairs, her thick brown hair bunched into a carelessly plaited ponytail, swinging from side to side down her back.

'No lift?'

'Electricity's out again.'

Sarah was strong and big-boned, with an open face. Assessing her as a woman, rather than as his little sister, Lev saw a sexually aggressive female in her handsome prime. He wondered how it was with Bruno. It would need to be good, to contain a woman like his sister. Perhaps she took lovers.

'Come up Lev. Come up. Don't just stand there in the dark. You must be tired, poor thing. How was your journey? Was customs a drag? They're right to be careful though. The water's hot and I've made a few of the things you used to like for you to eat – though I expect your tastes have changed after all this time. I can easily make something else. Only one more floor Lev. I'm on the third. I'm sorry about the elevator. It doesn't happen often. That it should happen the day you come! We've got lights in the flat though. Will you want a rest before you eat? Or do you want to eat after your shower? I'm sorry it's not a bath. Only a shower closet I'm afraid, that's all there's room for. And I've only the sofa in the sitting room for you to sleep on. I'm sorry. Are you wondering about Bruno? Don't. We can get to that later. Terrible about Dad. Only to be expected of course. He'd had one stroke already. About two months ago. Such a will, that man. He tried to walk but could only stumble. Tried to talk but could only mumble.'

She laughed nervously, startled at her unexpected couplet, her hand to her mouth. They were in her sitting room now. She had dumped his bags on the floor beside a little table that Lev thought he recognised.

'Used to be in Mum's sewing room. Don't you remember? Dad let me have it. He could be very kind sometimes. It was quick at the end, thank goodness. He would have hated to have hung on disabled. You must know all about strokes and things, the job you do. I bet you're a good doctor Lev, I could never be a doctor. I helped at the local hospital last year after that bombing near the bus station, they needed volunteers there were so many people hurt. Did you read about it? Did they bother to report it? So much of what happens here doesn't get reported. One Arab dies and it's front-page news across the world.'

The memory had surfaced too quickly; it had surprised her. She started to tremble and began gnawing away at her lower lip.

'Five dead, more than sixty injured. There was blood everywhere. The screaming was terrible. I'd never seen anything like it. Blood, screaming, flesh stripped off in sheets, mangled limbs, wounds so deep I saw bone. Headless trunks littering the corridor. It was sheer horror, Lev. Sheer horror. I've never experienced anything like the horror of the hospital that morning. A suicide bomber of course. They never look at you straight in the eye, Arabs. Do you remember how shifty and secretive they always are? What have we done to deserve such horror?'

'No one deserves it, Sarah, no one; whatever they may have done.'

'I was even asked to hold this woman down while they put stitches in her scalp. I thought I was going to be sick. I had the smell of blood on me for days – that's how it felt anyway.'

'It must have been awful for you'

'Yes well. I managed, didn't I?'

But then with hardly a pause she resumed as before, allowing no space for Lev to respond.

'How is it in London? Cold? Foggy? I'd love to see it at last. Perhaps I will now Dad's gone. Nobody to stop me now, is there? I expect Udi'd make a fuss. We'll have to see. He'll just have to put up with it. I've had one father, I don't need another. He gets so annoyed if I cross him. He has things on his mind though; I don't think it's very good between him and Leah. No children, you see, that's the problem. She's got nothing to do. She goes to London quite often, comes back loaded with clothes she doesn't need. And Udi's always buzzing off here and there too – on deals, so he tells me. A friend of mine saw him in Eilat with a woman in a restaurant. I didn't ask him about it, might hear something I don't want to. And then how could I look Leah squarely in the face? Before you ask, it's all over between Bruno and me. We can— oh but I've said that already.'

Lev put his hand on his sister's shoulder. She flinched

'You're right, border control was a drag. I'd love a shower. I'd like to eat as well. So after I've eaten, showered and changed into clean clothes, we can open a bottle of wine and talk properly. We can catch up, Sarah.'

'I'd like that Lev. I'd like that very much.' She hugged him. 'I'm so glad you're here.'

She stepped back and put her hands on her hips and looked at him.

'You're much thinner than you used to be. No bad thing for a man of your age I suppose.' Her eyes looked mildly amused. 'Much thinner on top too I see.'

Lev found himself anxiously patting the top of his head.

'Is it that thin?'

Again her hand went briefly to her mouth.

'I haven't upset you have I?'

'No, Sarah. No of course you haven't.'

'After all you are over forty now, aren't you? What do you expect? Goodness how time flies! You actually look very lean and fit these days Lev. And your London haircut does the world for your balding pate.' She giggled. 'Now. Are you sure you don't want to ring Udi? Perhaps you should. What do you think? I didn't tell him what time you would be arriving, so he won't be expecting you to ring – well, he'll be expecting it I think, but not at any particular time. I didn't really know what time you would arrive, how could I? So I've not been hiding anything from him, have I?'

She stopped talking and looked anxious suddenly. Before Lev could reassure her that she had no reason to feel any guilt about not contacting Udi, she plunged on.

'Did you have a nice trip? You were very mysterious about how you were getting here. Did you fly direct to Ben Gurion? Knowing what you're like, I expect you didn't. Should I get his number? Udi's I mean. Now where is my little address book? It's red. Have you seen it anywhere? No, of course you haven't, you've only just got here. I can never quite remember his number. He insists on getting me to call him on his mobile. I don't know why. Leah's always on the landline I suppose. And it is such a long number. I just can't remember it. What did Dad used to say? "You don't have to remember what you know where to look up" – something like that, wasn't it? Don't you remember?'

Lev shook his head.

'You don't? He was always coming out with little sayings, especially towards the end. Now where is that book? It must be somewhere about. Dad used to say that if my head were separate from my body I'd lose it. When his speech really deteriorated, his sayings were all I could understand. Poor Dad.'

She was becoming tearful again so he hugged her tight. She clung on hard.

'Sarah.'

'Yes?'

He spoke very softly. 'I don't want speak to Udi tonight. I want a shower and something to eat, then I want to talk to you, catch up. And I've got to get this cleaned up, too.'

He showed her his hand.

'What happened? How did you get that?'

'Climbing through the barrier at Abou Dis.'

'You came through Abou Dis!'

'I did.'

'But why? Nobody goes there now. They say it's risky. I suppose you didn't realise. Well at least you're here now, safe and sound.'

'Sarah?'

'Yes Lev?'

'Where's this shower of yours?'

✳ ✳ ✳

An hour later Lev was sitting in the corner of Sarah's sofa with a glass of red wine, clean and fed.

'Rather good this.'

'From Dad's cellar. I went and fetched a few bottles when it was decided I was going to look after him here, after his first stroke. I thought he might like a glass occasionally.'

'You looked after him while he was ill?'

'I did.'

'Here?'

'Yes.'

'That explains it.'

'Explains what?'

'The policeman who checked my passport downstairs in the street appeared to know Dad very well. How long was he here? Quite a long time by the sound of it.'

'Over a month. Perhaps six weeks. You seem surprised.'

'I suppose I'd assumed that you'd get in a nurse. Wouldn't he have preferred to have been in his own house?'

'I think he would, yes. But Udi thought it would all cost too much money. More than he wanted to spend. And I didn't want to go and live in the old house. Since Mum died, and then you went and left.' She hesitated. 'Sorry, Lev, but you know what I mean.'

'That's all right, Sarah. Don't worry.'

'Anyway, it's very cold and draughty there now – and frankly quite depressing. Dad had done nothing to brighten it up for years. So, since Udi thought it would be a good opportunity to get it done up a bit, and since I work from home now and need to be here to take calls, Dad came and lived with me. A physio called everyday to take him through his exercises. She took him for walks occasionally. He couldn't manage very far. I think he was happy enough, and I quite enjoyed looking after him.'

'Did Dad ask for it to be done up?'

'The house? No, Udi just thought it would be a good idea.'

'What, as a surprise for Dad for when he got better?'

'No, to prepare it for sale.'

'Why? Dad was still alive!'

'Udi wanted to get an estimate of how much it might fetch.'

His sister looked uncomfortable suddenly.

'Sarah is something going on? What's he up to?'

'Nothing Lev, nothing.'

'It sounds to me like Udi is up to something.'

'Can we talk about it tomorrow? It's late, and you must be tired. Want some coffee? A cigarette?'

'I'd love one. You don't mind? In your flat I mean.'

'Lots of my men friends smoke. I might even join you, I have the occasional one myself these days. Don't look so shocked. I'll get the coffee.'

Lev closed his eyes briefly. He was tired now. A cigarette and some coffee would wake him up. There was obviously a lot to talk over.

'What happened with Bruno?'

'Bruno? In short, we both had an affair. He found out about mine and he left.'

'Just like that?'

'Pretty much. I should never have married him. I'm sure it was only because you left that I married him anyway.'

Lev was silent.

'You may think that's nonsense but it's true. I realised pretty soon that it had been a mistake. Too late then, more's the pity. The atmosphere was hell after you went, everyone trying to avoid talking about you – especially in front of Dad. That's another reason why I don't like the old house anymore, even now. It was a miserable place to live. I wanted a life of my own, and marriage was the simplest way out for a good Jewish girl. Bruno was one of Udi's friends from his army days. Do you remember him?'

'Not really.'

'Udi brought him home a couple of times, probably when you were at medical school. Dad always liked him. Quite good looking, in a military sort of way. Lots of my friends fancied him. Bit of a catch really, I suppose. It was all very easy. His family's got money, they promised us a house for a wedding present, so we got married. But it was difficult from the off. He wasn't much fun, and I think he thought I was a bit empty-headed. We struggled on for quite a while. Children would have made a difference probably. Usually do.'

'Might have trapped you in a joyless marriage.'

'Perhaps, but Bruno really wanted a family. I would have become a Jewish mother wouldn't I? He may have held me in slightly higher regard. But they didn't come.'

'Are you seeing anyone special now?'

'No. I'm playing the field and it's quite fun. It was a bit difficult while Dad was here but I managed. He slept in my room. Slept pretty deeply most nights thank goodness. That's how I know the sofa's comfortable.'

She grinned mischievously.

'And your affair?'

'Oh that.'

'You don't have to tell me about it if you don't want to.'

'No it's alright. Do you remember Rachel Sahed? I went to school with her.'

'Vaguely.'

'Well we've stayed good friends. She is in a "joyless marriage", as you call it, too. No children again. She married into pots of money. Sadly, Malkiel, her husband, is really a very tedious man. A good man but terribly tedious. His family is from Hungary. Originally they were tradesmen, painters and decorators. They started buying up old property, converting and modernising and then selling on. They made a lot of money, his father especially. Malkiel's a bit idle. He and Rachel live off the millions. This flat was one of theirs – I got it at a good price because I was so close to Rachel. She and I started going to the gym together. Afterwards we'd sit over coffee, moaning about our husbands. Well, not to put too fine a point on it, she had a little private session with our instructor – a moment of weakness – and couldn't stop going on about how great it was. A revelation, she called it. So when the opportunity arose I had a moment of weakness of my

own. And he was quite something I can tell you. Boring as
hell afterwards, but you can't have everything can you?
About as deep as a puddle, sadly.'

Lev laughed. 'And Bruno found out?'

'Yes. I don't quite know how, but everyone knows each
other's business, especially among the old families, so I suppose it wasn't surprising. I found out later that he'd been
having a relationship with his business partner's sister for
most of the time we were married. Anyway he's living with
her now in our little house. That's why I'm here in this
rabbit hutch.'

Lev looked around the room. The flat occupied half of a
much larger original one. Its tiny hallway was screened
from the main room by a red and green bead curtain. The
main room itself was square, with a small balcony. There
were two low modern sofas of chrome and white mock
leather, and between them a rug with a faint geometric
design, over linoleum with a pattern that was supposed to
look like floorboards. Surrounded by five chairs was a plain
wooden table, which, at a squeeze, could seat six. The glass
door onto the balcony, and the window that ran the length
of it, were the room's only source of daylight. On the wall
beside the bead curtain was an oval mirror, but there were
no pictures. The mirror, like the table below it, was from
their mother's sewing room. The kitchen and the bath-
room were no more than large walk-in cupboards, separated from the main room by simple stud walls. The room
where Sarah slept was as it had been before Malkiel's con-
version, and hinted at the generous proportions of the original apartment.

'You didn't ever mention any of this in your letters.'

'It was all a bit tawdry. I suppose also I was ashamed at the mess I'd made.'

'It happens.'

'Not to a daughter of Levi Dubnow it doesn't.'

'How did he take it?'

'With resignation. He was more disappointed in Bruno than he was in me. We did eventually talk about it. He thought Bruno had behaved dishonourably.'

'And what's all this about you never seeing me again? You could have always jumped on a plane and come to London. It's not much more than four hours away. Visited me. You know, like people do.'

'Dad forbade us to, don't you remember?'

'How could I forget?'

'And Bruno wouldn't have wanted me to either.'

'I see. Was his opinion so important?'

'He was my husband. Of course it was important.'

'OK, but you could have lied and said you were going somewhere else.'

'Yes, I could have lied. I did consider it but I would have been in so much trouble if anyone had found out. And more than that, it would have upset Dad terribly if he had got to hear of it. He was an old man, Lev. Why should I have risked causing him all that distress?'

'Why? Well, I'm tempted say that you should have risked distressing him for me.'

'Why should I have done that? You were the one that left after all, you were the one that deserted.'

'That damn word again.'

'What word?'

'*Deserted.*'

'But it's what you did, Lev, totally and finally. It was as if you had walked out and closed the door and we had all ceased to exist the moment the latch clicked.'

'I wrote.'

'I wrote first, Lev Dubnow. I wonder sometimes whether I'd have ever heard from you again if I hadn't.'

Lev was silent.

'When you left, did you stop for even one brief moment to consider us, any of us, me? Well did you?'

She has to say what she has to say, thought Lev. Better out than in. But she had let him leave, hadn't she? She hadn't protested, or remonstrated with Dad or Udi.

'No, of course you didn't,' she continued. 'You just wanted to get out, however much misery you caused. You just wanted your Jo, and to hell with the rest of us. Some might say you were lucky to have experienced such love and tenderness. On good days I might even agree with them – it was on those days that I brought up the possibility of making some sort of contact with you. But everyone said you'd have changed, that it wouldn't be welcome. I didn't need much convincing. Udi said we were an embarrassment to you, that you hated even being a Jew. He said you'd probably change your name to Joanna's. Dr Payne. You didn't change your name, did you Lev?'

'Of course I didn't.'

'I wasn't sure about Joanna, either.'

'I don't know why. You two always got on OK. She would have loved you to come. I always half expected you to.'

'Really?'

Lev looked down at his coffee.

'Although Jo said you wouldn't. She didn't believe that

you would be strong enough to disappoint Dad or defy Udi. And as it turned out she was right wasn't she? Perhaps she understood, bless her, better than I did, the power of it all – the magnitude, in your eyes, of what I'd done. She used to say it was nothing to do with me personally, that it was all to do with Israel. Dad accused her of deriding his beliefs, and she may have. But she also completely understood his attachment to the land, what it all meant to him, how deep it all went. "Down to his very marrow", she used to say.'

'I was never certain that she liked me very much.'

'She liked you well enough but she did think you should have been more aware of how everything was here. Jo was impatient with you. If you had come, she would have welcomed you. She would certainly have been pleased for me – she would have made you feel welcome for that reason alone.'

'So what actually happened between you? Was it to do with losing the baby?'

'Partly. And all the blame attached.' Lev grimaced and shrugged his shoulders, then took a sip from his coffee and lit a cigarette. 'I think I bored her actually, after a while. We should have gone back to London to have the baby. Bloody Boer doctor. We argued about that constantly afterwards. There was also my guilt about you and the family. Especially after your letters started arriving. The daily grind of work finally took its toll, too. All those things. And she found me less exciting in London than she did here. She had the idea that I'd used her as an excuse to get out of Israel, to get away from Udi. There may be some truth in that as well, as it happens. About Udi I mean. I tried not to think about Israel, tried not to talk much about it. That in itself exasperated her.

"Insufferably passive", she used to call me. I was too serious; she was too irreverent about things that I valued. We came from two such contrasting cultures. That should have been exciting and stimulating, but it just made things difficult. I'd dread hearing about what was happening in Israel. She'd get so angry. She'd say that I didn't care enough. She was right, I didn't. Finally, I wasn't quite good enough as I was. There was too much in me she disliked. So she gave herself to someone else. A musician. Charmed her with his lyre I expect. I did hear just before I left that it hasn't lasted – he's moved out apparently. I'll deal with that when I get back, if there is anything to deal with. Is that enough for you?' Lev shrugged his shoulders and cleared his throat. 'Too many cigarettes. Now, let me see how comfortable this sofa really is.'

He laughed briefly then looked out through the balcony window into the darkness. 'At least Jo and I parted before we began hating each other. It is such a waste of what's gone before when that happens. Bitterness has a wretched habit of burying happy memories, don't you think?'

He fingered his brow. 'See you in the morning little sister.'

Sarah got up to go to her room. 'Goodnight Lev. Are you sure you'll be comfortable enough?'

'This is fine.'

He looked up at her, his eyes small and empty, all light gone.

He had lost himself in Joanna, had felt such overwhelming love for her that he had been strengthened and energised, made a more aware and generous person. He had experienced real joy, an unalloyed joy, for the first time since his mother's death. But despite its intensity, their love had been easy and carefree; there had been laughter as well as tenderness. Joanna's interest in every detail of life made life more worthwhile; every event, however small, became important and significant. He had consciously cherished every moment. And when it all collapsed? There was a sadness that for a few days bordered on depression; then an achingly oppressive emptiness, a depthless void that had to be filled. It was then that he had that fleeting relationship with Robin James, a mistake, a needless and careless mistake.

In the end he was simply grateful. He fully realised how fortunate he had been that his relationship with Joanna had happened at all, and realised, too, that it had left him with a precious legacy: if ever anything like it was to occur again he would have the capacity to recognise it for what it was, to understand the importance of it and grasp it even more fiercely and fearlessly than he had with her.

∗ ∗ ∗

Lev was awake early. He was disappointed to see that the sky was grey. There was a wind as well. He padded across the room and let himself out on to the balcony. It was chilly; the faint orb of the sun, glowing through thin cloud, was still low. The air tasted dusty. He shivered. The street below was still quiet. As he turned to go back in, he heard the faint sound of a single muezzin's call from the Old City. Then he heard another, then another, and yet another, until there was an uneven chorus, clear and distinct, imposing itself on the early morning silence, demanding to be heard.

'I hate that sound.' Sarah had come out on to the balcony, wrapped tight in a faded pink dressing-gown. She was gnawing her lower lip again. 'You're up early, Lev. Can't sleep?'

'Have I disturbed you? I was trying to be quiet.'

'No, not all. Since I've lived alone I always seem to wake more or less with the sun.'

'You and me both.'

'You were an early riser as a child, I seem to remember. Dad used to say you'd make a good soldier.'

Lev laughed.

'Breakfast?'

'Just coffee. Strong coffee and a fag is how I start my day.'

'Very healthy.'

Sarah went into her kitchen. Lev leant against the wall in the kitchen doorway and watched his sister. It was a tiny space.

'How do you do your washing? Do you have to go to the launderette?'

'I go once a week. There's no room for a washing machine in here. Why? Do you want washing done? We can easily drop it off. I know the woman there. If she gets it before ten, she has it done by four. She's very good. Takes great care.'

'I've no washing to be done, don't worry.'

Lev drifted back onto the balcony.

'There must be a storm in the Negev.'

'That's what Dad used to say. Is the air dusty outside? Can you feel it on your lips?'

'I can. Gritty and bitter.'

'There'll be rain today then.'

'Do you think so?'

'Probably,' she said, handing him a cup of coffee.

'Is it a free day we have before us or have you something arranged?'

'No, I've not arranged anything, but I should contact Udi

– as indeed you should – if only to enquire whether he wants any help with anything.'

'Leave that until this afternoon. If you think it's going to rain let's get out and about before it does. Why don't we spend the morning in the Old City?'

'Now there's somewhere I haven't been for a long time.'

'All the better. We can stroll and chat, have a tea here and there. Wander around, see how it's changed. Are you up for that?'

'I'd love to but I do feel guilty about leaving everything to Leah and Udi. There's a lot to be done for Dad's party. We've decided to provide a meal. I should see what I can do to help.'

'Are you catering? Is that usual for these sort of occasions?'

'Leah thought it was appropriate. She arranged it all. Some of the old boys have come from abroad to attend and they're really quite ancient, some of them. They'll need some sustenance just to keep going. We don't want anyone keeling over.'

'Sounds as if you need a couple of ambulance crews hanging around.'

'Apparently Leah has organised that too.'

'Has she? Well, I'm sure she's got everything completely under control and has absolutely no need of you.'

'I suppose you're right.'

'Of course I am. Go on, go and get dressed. I might even buy you a new dressing gown. That thing's seen better days. Something gold and gaudy like Arab women wear.'

She laughed.

'I don't think so.'

He could see she was pleased.

✳ ✳ ✳

They were out of the flat by nine. A taxi slowed expectantly in front of them as they came out onto the street, the driver gently sounding his horn. Lev waved him away.

'Let's walk shall we? Cut up into Jaffa Road and down to the Old City that way? Alright with you?'

'Fine. Whatever. I'll follow you. Can you remember the way?'

'We'll soon see won't we? I think so.'

Lev found his way to Jaffa Road without any trouble.

'What's that all about? Over there Sarah. Look.'

Across the street, with their backs against a shop window, were seven teenage boys in a line, eyes on the pavement, hands in pockets. One or two of them were impatiently scuffing at the ground. Facing them with the barrels of their guns pointing directly at them were four young soldiers – two boys and two girls. A jeep, its blue lights flashing, was parked a few yards down the road, causing an obstruction. The traffic had to edge its way past. It was rush hour and a queue of vehicles was beginning to grow in both directions.

'Security Lev. Just security.'

One of the girls, tall, slim and completely aware of her good looks, was collecting ID cards, her beret perched to one side on top of a mound of fair, tightly curling hair. When she had finished, without looking at either the cards or the boys, she sauntered back to her mates and handed the cards to the other girl, who, together with one of the boy soldiers, began to inspect each card one by one, glancing from time to time at the line, checking photographs with faces. The fourth young soldier, asthmatically thin and pale, with a light blue yarmulke clipped carelessly on the back of his head, lit a cigarette and wandered back to the jeep, jumping into the passenger seat. The inspection over, the other boy, a big muscular lad with a crewcut, followed him and sat behind the wheel. Revving the engine into a roar, he flicked on his indicators and let the engine idle. He took a drag of his companion's cigarette. The traffic had stopped altogether now, in anticipation of the jeep taking off up the street. It didn't.

Meanwhile the two girls were waving their guns at the boys, getting them to space themselves out at arm's length from each other. One was a little slower than the rest and the slim girl stepped forward and pointed her gun directly at him. He glared at her defiantly but sidestepped smartly into place. She wasn't satisfied, and before he could drop his eyes moodily to the ground, she gestured with her gun for him to separate himself further from the boy on his left, which meant in turn that the other three on his right had to move again. She then made a few further adjustments. When she was finally satisfied, she turned back to her friend. The second girl was short and fat, her hair a dull brown. The jeep was still idling and the traffic queues were getting longer.

'They're no more than children.'

'Who?'

'The soldiers. And the boys they've stopped, if it comes to that. What are they supposed to have done do you think?'

'They are Arabs Lev. They are obviously on their way to the Old City, and they're in a Jewish area. They need to be checked.'

'Is that all?'

'It's very important.'

'I'm sure it is, but it looks to me like that there's a little bit of gratuitous intimidation going on as well. Are they supposed to be terrorists, these Arab boys?'

'We have to be careful. They hate us, these people. They are always looking for an opportunity to hurt us. They could be carrying arms.'

'Carrying arms? You're joking, surely. Their clothes are so tight and shoddy I can see the cigarette packet in that little one's trouser pocket. And anyway, how are you so certain they are Arabs?'

'Don't be silly, Lev. You can see they are.'

'Can you? You mean they're shifty looking, like all Arabs? Is that what you mean?'

'Don't be a pain. Come on, we were going to have a nice morning out and about, remember?'

'Just wait a minute, I want to see what happens.'

'You'll get noticed, Lev, and then you'll get checked as well. You have got your passport on you I hope?'

'Wouldn't go anywhere without it.'

The girls were now looking at the ID cards a second time, matching photographs with faces again. This time though they were pointing at one or two of the boys individually, clearly appraising them, giggling to each other as they did so. They called out names so that the boys concerned looked up at them. One even began to preen a little when he realised he had particularly caught their attention.

'Come on Lev. We must get on.'

'Wait a moment more. Let's see how this all turns out.'

Eventually the girl who had originally collected the cards stepped forward and beckoned the handsome lad towards her, stopping him a couple of feet away from her by brandishing her weapon in his face. She asked him his name; he told her. She sifted through the cards in her hand until she found his. She then looked him slowly up and down, comparing what she saw with the photograph on his card. Then she appeared to look with amusement, even mockery, straight into his eyes, holding his gaze until he was finally forced to lower it to the ground at her feet. As he did so, he dropped his head too. Only then did she offer his card back to him – but in such a way that he had to stretch forward to grasp hold of it. She had made it very clear that he should-n't step any closer to her.

'Sarah this little pantomime is really nasty. It is nothing less than public sexual humiliation.'

At last she casually pointed her gun over her shoulder and he slouched off with his hands in his pockets and his ID card between his gritted teeth. Slowly, she repeated the exercise with each of the others until they were all gone. Game over, she skipped back to her friend and they both ran laughing to the jeep. The engine roared, the siren was switched on, and, performing a sweeping u-turn between the queuing vehicles, it shot off up the hill, forcing the waiting cars to pull in sharply to let it through.

There had been no conversation, just orders and gestures. Neither the soldiers nor the boys had made any attempt to communicate or interact.

'It's as if both parties were determined to maintain a barrier. If they'd made the effort to speak to each other, they may have found they have more in common than they think. People who are used to having servants always claim that they have to maintain a boundary that must never be crossed.'

'Absolutely right. How else can we make sure we retain their respect? They have to know their place.'

'Except those Arab boys are not our servants, are they Sarah?'

'Yes but—'

'But what?'

'We control things here and anything that muddies that just causes trouble.'

All this time a mobile blood transfusion team had been processing a little queue of donors. Another line of people, chatting agreeably, was now waiting to be registered at a collapsible desk by a woman of Sarah's age, with similarly, and just as carelessly, bunched thick hair dangling down her back, 'pioneer style'.

'Come on, Lev. Seen enough now?'. The routine was proceeding as though nothing untoward had occurred.

'This sort of thing happens all the time, I can see. No one around that trailer noticed a thing.'

'They're busy, Lev.'

'You reckon the Arabs want to hurt you Sarah. I'm not surprised. I'd want to hurt you, if I'd just been subjected to something like that.'

'We mustn't give them the chance then must we? We have to convince these people that they won't get away with it if they hurt us. If the only thing that convinces them is humiliation then that's what we'll do. It is entirely up to them. Three or four years ago, as Jews, we'd have been scurrying around on the rooftop walkways. Oh yes, there is a whole network of open paths up there above the souks. In those days Jews felt too at risk walking through a street full of Arabs.'

They walked along in grim silence up the hill. The Arab

boys were up ahead of them now, crossing the road at the traffic lights, before going down the path to the Jaffa Gate entrance to the Old City.

'Look at those boys Sarah. Look at them hard for God's sake.'

'Don't get so angry Lev. You sound like Udi. I'm looking. I'm looking. What am I supposed to see?'

'Look at their posture. It oozes resentment and hostility. And I bet they left home an hour or so ago full of high spirits, looking forward to a morning around town, just as we did.'

Lev and Sarah passed under the first arch of Jaffa Gate. Sarah grazed the tips of her fingers across the black steel mezuzah and put them to her lips. Turning sharply through the second arch, they arrived in a bright little square. It was still windy, and becoming slowly colder. There were a few drops of rain, as Sarah had predicted.

'My God, just look at this place.'

'Look at what, Lev? You're getting just a tiny bit tiresome.'

'The place is heaving with guns. Soldiers there. Police there. And more soldiers and more police. And they've all got guns.'

'I don't notice anymore. I'm so used it.'

'You wouldn't be if you got stopped all the time.'

'I do get stopped. I get stopped quite often. Some of them dress up like us you see.'

'Oh do they? What impudence! I need to sit down. Have a break from all this misery. Get a cup of coffee. What about this place? I know it, actually – I used to meet Jo here sometimes. It was nice and quiet, if a bit shabby and dingy.'

Just as he was about to go in and find a table, Lev stopped and pointed towards the end of the square. 'Not again. Those kids are being checked again, Sarah. Over there, look. Those poor lads.'

The men who were checking them had rifles and revolvers like the police and soldiers but weren't wearing uniforms.

'It's alright Lev. Those particular men who're checking them out aren't interested in small fry like your beloved Arab boys.'

'Who are they then? Come to think of it, I saw some like them at the border.'

'Internal Security. I think that's what they call them. I get confused, there are so many different forces and squads responsible for this and that: internal, external, border, national. It's a wonder they can think up names for them all. Anyway there must be some important VIP visiting the Old City, that's why everything coming through the gate is being stopped. Usually it's just the odd car, but they're even checking cars with Israeli plates today.'

The boys were let go after a couple of quick questions and were now disappearing down into the Bazaar.

'I don't know how you can live like this.'

'As I said before, you'll get used it.'

'I don't want to get used to this. I can't be bothered with coffee. Let's get on.'

At the far end of the square was a little lane that plunged steeply down into the Old City.

It was all very much as Lev remembered.

The sky was barely visible between overhanging awnings, in places vanishing altogether. On either side of the lane, crammed in tight together, were little souvenir shops – some no more than kiosks, some resembling huge warrens, burrowing deep into the ground among ancient stones that had probably been there since Solomon's time. Naked light bulbs dangled brightly not far above head-height. Branching off here and there were other lanes and alleys, some so narrow people had to squeeze against each other to pass; some like great arched avenues; others seeming to disappear into a brightly-illuminated distance; still others leading to closed doors. The goods in the shops overflowed onto the walkway to such an extent that it was sometimes almost impossible to pass, and the steps and ramps which had been installed to help pedestrians negotiate the slope instead made walking a stumbling, spine-jarring experience.

As Lev and Sarah passed an alley hanging with bloody carcasses ready for the butcher's knife, a crocodile of school children in green and white knee-length tunics and dark blue long trousers filed up towards them, armed blue-shirted security guards in front and behind. Blank opaque sunglasses masked the guards' eyes, and their clean-shaven heads shone under the lights.

The shopkeepers' calls had not changed much either. 'Hallo, hallo. Come into my shop. One minute, one minute. Welcome, welcome. My friend, my friend. Not buy, just look. No price for looking. You come back later? See what I have. No business today. Take my card. Later? See you later. I wait for you.'

'Quite a few places are closed.'

'Since the latest intafada the tourists have stopped coming. Some of the shopkeepers are forced to sell off their stock at low prices just to keep some money coming in. Apparently there's some really valuable old stuff in some of these crummy little shops, if you know what you're looking for. A good time to buy. I have some friends who do. They're making quite a killing.'

She pointed to a neat, clean lane to their right.

'Western Wall?'

'Why not?'

They turned into the lane, took a left down some steps and then right again down a small slope. Here it was quiet and clean after the dirt and noise of the market. At the bottom of the slope was a glass box the size of a freight container. There were police inside: a very dark, African-looking girl with delicate features, and a tall boy with bold, friendly eyes behind little square glasses. Both were armed and wore bulletproof jackets. The boy greeted them warmly.

'How yer doin'? Great! Bags through here, you through there.'

The girl gestured Lev to go through a metal detector and then silently brushed a handheld device up and down his body. Sarah followed him through the same procedure. Meanwhile the tall boy looked intently at his screen as their bags slid through the baggage scan. Satisfied, he looked up at them.

'Thanks folks. Have a good day.'

'She was very serious,' said Lev as they walked away.

'The Ethiopian? She has to be, she's got an important job. You see Lev, we are searched as well as everyone else.'

'How did you know she was Ethiopian?'

'It was obvious.'

As Sarah and Lev emerged, a group of rowdy boys in black suits and hats, with little beards that barely concealed their chins, pushed past and bustled through the guard post. The two young guards didn't even look up. It seemed to Lev they shied away from taking them on.

'*They weren't!*'

'Weren't what?'

'Checked.'

He looked at his sister and gave her a quick hug. Sarah was touchingly flustered.

'They were leaving. It's only those coming in who have to be checked.'

'Those two wouldn't have dreamt of checking that particular group of young men, whichever way they were going, I'd put money on it.'

They walked down some wide white stone steps that Lev didn't remember being there before, and out on to the square. The Western Wall towered above them: prayer sheets and messages, stuffed in between its ancient stones, fluttered and snapped in the swirling breeze that had been growing in sharpness all morning.

Lev held back.

'You're not coming?'

'No Sarah, you go ahead.'

He watched her push her way through the crowds into the section set aside for women and children.

Lev and his brother used to come to this sacred place with their father when they were small. As they had grown older their father had tended to go alone, the brothers managing to find some excuse for not going with him. The place had disconcerted Lev as a child, and it disconcerted him now. He had hardly been a participant – more his father's companion – but nevertheless he was troubled by the murmurous fervour of the worshipers around him, and the colossal height of the wall which seemed about to fall and crush him. And then there was his father standing beside him in a state of trance-like ecstasy. It troubled Lev, and frightened him too. He had since been to other sacred places, places where for centuries people had gathered to pray, a few of which had so much palpable energy that the atmosphere was almost feverish – infectious, contractible. Benares, Lourdes. In those very few places he had felt very clearly the frailty of his sanity, realised how close the border was between sound sense, reason and the other side. He had no clear idea what the other side was like – how could he? He had not been there – but he was aware enough of its proximity, and frightened enough of what it might be like, not to risk going there. Lev withdrew into himself. These intensely holy places intimidated him.

*'The divine presence is here Lev, in these great stones. The first and second temples may have been desecrated and destroyed but their presence, their holiness remains. Look up, Lev. Look up to the top. Higher, Lev, higher. They were there, high above you. Lament their loss my son. Lament their loss and then, in your prayers, demand their replacement. Kiss the stones, press your forehead against them Lev. Add your faith to the faith of the millions that have gone before you. Make yourself one with the divinity of this place. For years we were denied ready access. We will not be deprived again. You and I will die rather than allow that to happen. And then in time the third temple will be built up there, high up there above you, on the sacred site of Aravna's threshing floor.'*

'Are you OK?' Sarah had returned.

'Yes fine. Do you mind if we go now?'

'No of course not.'

'Do you still believe in all this stuff?'

'Of course. Is it lost to you completely?'

'For the most part. I'm sorry, Sarah. I must be a disappointment to you. I was to him, wasn't I?'

'Dad you mean.'

'Who else? And I do think I believed in it all at one time, everything he told me. He did, didn't he – absolutely?'

'Yes Lev, he did.'

'Let's go home. You should ring Udi. I'll come out again this afternoon and mooch around for a bit on my own.'

'Will you go to the grave?'

'Perhaps on the morning of the grand gathering. What time does it begin?'

'About midday.'

'I'll have time that morning then, won't I?'

'You should at least speak to Udi on the telephone beforehand.'

'I don't think I can quite face our brother yet. Not even on the telephone. I'm sorry, Sarah.'

'It's up to you, Lev.'

'Thanks. What exactly is Udi up to with Dad's house? You never did get round to it last night.'

* * *

Lev wanted to return to the Old City. The morning had done nothing for his spirits. Apprehensive about returning to Israel anyway, the episode on Jaffa Road had troubled him in an unexpected way, as had his sister's defence of the soldiers' behaviour. That afternoon Lev took a different route, down Ben Yehuda, and through on to Hillel. As he climbed Shlomo Hamelech the huge crenellated walls of the Old City towered up over the horizon. The view down to Jaffa Gate and the Citadel beyond was impressive, he thought, without being actually beautiful. The clouds had gone completely and the sun was warm for the first time that day. To enjoy the brightness and comforting warmth, he sat down for a few moments on a stone bench under the walls, just outside the shadow of the gate. Sharing the bench with him was a group of boys between twelve and fourteen years old.

They were playing the fool like kids of that age everywhere – full of themselves and self-conscious at being free to do as they pleased, but keenly aware of their youth in a place where adults were in charge. To hide their awkwardness they displayed themselves to each other, yelling and shouting, singing pop songs and dancing about. They laughed and nudged each other when girls walked by, and occasionally, out of bravado, called out to them. An old Sephardi hurried by and looked across at them with guarded irritation. They called after him too. What they called, Lev couldn't quite catch. Having grown up without much contact with Arab children, his knowledge of Arabic had never been very profound – and being told that they smelt hadn't encouraged him to make any sort of relationship with those he occasionally met.

One of the boys suddenly ran to the corner of a wall, crouching down behind it before leaping out and swinging his arm up in an arched movement, as if he was throwing a grenade at the departing Jew's back. Not content with that, he began to mime the firing of a round from an imaginary M16, his fresh young features contorted into an unpleasant grimace, teeth bared. The other boys had stood up and were stamping and hooting with laughter. The play over, he

sauntered back to his rapturous audience with a smirk of a
job well done and sat down. At first merely interested by the
boy's playacting, Lev had been chilled by his intense expression. The rest of his act may have been mimicry, but what
spontaneously appeared on his face was real enough. The
other boys settled themselves down next to him and they all
began to talk quietly to each other.

After only a few minutes – restless perhaps, now that the
sudden excitement was over – they stood up and began to
stroll up the hill. It was as if Lev had been invisible. They
hadn't once shown any sign that they were aware of his
presence.

Out of the shadow of the great square gate came two
other boys, only a few years older than the ones who had
just been sitting beside Lev but they wore yarmulkas and
were armed. They shouted at the group to stop, which the
boys did, looking round to see who was calling. The mimic
was beckoned to come back down the hill. When the rest of
the group appeared to be following, they were warned to
stay where they were. They stood about moodily, murmur-
ing to each other, watchful and suspicious. Lev noticed
again the strange beckoning gesture he had seen earlier
that day, and at the border the day before: knuckles were
bared in the direction of those being called and then the
hand, usually the right, was slowly opened and shut into a
loose fist, thumb out wide as if about to hitch a ride. To stop
the person approaching, a flat palm was shown. In London
during a demonstration that Joanna had insisted Lev
attend with her, a policeman had beckoned him by simply
curling and uncurling an index finger while cocking one
eye. Lev had felt apprehensive, but no more than if he had

been a small boy about to be told off. The knuckle-bared gesture seemed to him much more significant and threatening. Implicit in it was something infinitely more dangerous than just a ticking off. He presumed that there was a whole range of possible consequences for what the kids had done. The uncertainty about which one might or might not be imposed on this particular occasion would have added to their apprehension.

The two Israelis halted the boy just short of arm's length away from them. He had come watchfully, pulling his ID card out of the back pocket of his jeans. The two young Jews were shorter than he was and jerked their chins up at him as they spoke, in an effort to impose their authority. They needn't have bothered. He was cowed and sullenly passive, his shoulders hunched in an attempt to diminish and protect himself. Having checked his card, they motioned for him to step to one side. They walked in front of him, putting themselves between him and his companions, and called the rest of the group using the same strange hand gesture. Each boy was warily alert as one by one they obeyed.

Having checked the rest of the ID cards, one of the Israelis put them in his trouser pocket, nestled his gun into the crook of his arm and together with his colleague walked off up the hill. Neither of them bothered to look back, confident the group had no choice but to follow. As they trailed up the hill in the wake of the two young Jews, the boys flung furtive glances around, checking to see if anybody was watching. One of them caught sight of Lev and glared at him. His look smouldered with anger rather than with resignation or defeat.

\* \* \*

Lev turned away towards the Old City. He passed through Jaffa Gate and across the square still full of police and soldiers, and down to the bazaar. Turning left into Christian Quarter Road, he walked past the alley that led to the Church of the Holy Sepulchre, then cut down through some side lanes until he found himself climbing the steps to another of the old entrances to the walled city, Damascus Gate. He couldn't remember when he had last come here. Probably with Joanna. She had loved dipping in and out of the narrow alleys and lanes, coming to dead ends, turning back and discovering some other way she hadn't found before. He had forgotten to call in at Moses' shop to see if the old jewellery-maker was still alive. As a present for Joanna, Lev had bought a Jerusalem Cross from Moses. It had four stones set among beautiful silver filigree and she used to hang it from a leather thong around her neck. Moses had been old then. Despite his age, he would sit all day making crosses, squinting through thick lenses to which were hinged green filters ready to be snapped down to protect his blood-shot eyes from the welding-flame he used to fuse the delicate strands of silver.

Lev was conscious suddenly that he had just walked through one of the most fascinating places on earth without seeing a thing. The boy's smouldering glare of fury had unsettled him; such an intense expression, he realised, had to have a consequence. For a ready smile to appear on that boy's face again, some penalty would have to be exacted.

Lev pulled himself together.

The Old City was a tight square kilometre of alleys and

lanes, steps and ramps, bazaars and markets; hidden homes clustered around tiny yards; patriarchal mansions behind high stone walls; churches, mosques and synagogues; seminaries and monasteries; domes, towers and minarets. Shops selling ancient Russian icons jostled with stalls selling cabbages, light bulbs with perfume, bloody carcasses with elegant hejebs, delicate Bedouin jewellery with shoddy jeans from Taiwan. Sheltering within its high Ottoman walls – thirty-two massive stones high in places – were some of the most sacred shrines of Judaism, Christianity and Islam. It slanted more or less from its northern walls to its south-eastern corner, where the Temple Mount and the Al-Aqsa Mosque rose above the Western Wall.

As Lev climbed north up the steep steps that led to Damascus Gate he was surrounded by traders selling from makeshift stalls, tables and sometimes just sheets on the ground. There were cages of live rabbits on one table, alongside another selling toy plastic M16s. As he came through the Gate there were yet more stalls, stretching up into a wide amphitheatre of a market, and threading east along the wall towards the next entrance, Herod's Gate. There were soap and tomatoes, perfume and cabbages, socks and coffee pots, carpets and oranges. Further on were falafel and shwarma stalls, and fruit-juice sellers crushing lemons, pomegranates and grapes fresh for each customer.

The scene around him began to lift his spirits, and he strolled on, feeling better. He bought some cigarettes from an upturned crate between a heap of huge cauliflowers and a table cluttered with blue and gold vases. Pushing his way through the crowds swirling out of Herod Gate after midday prayers at Al-Aqsa, he went into a coffee house. Inside were

tables of men drinking tea and playing cards and back-
gammon. The air was dense with cigarette and narghile
smoke.

He sat at a table by himself and ordered a tea. The just-
washed glass, when it arrived, left a wet mark on the table-
top. Lev felt a tap on his shoulder, and a man in a traditional Arab headdress warned him to be careful not to soil
his sleeve. Calling for a cloth, he wiped the wet mark dry
and with a brief smile returned to his card game.

Outside were torrents of people, surging up the hill from
worship. Prayer beads, cigarettes and bulging black plastic
bags hung from their fingers. There were men with men,
women with women, and small children hand in hand with
both men and women – but very few women and men
together. Most of the women wore cream-coloured hejebs;
occasionally an older woman wore white with little tassels. Lev
noticed that the younger the woman, the tighter the hejeb –
the teenage girls in short jackets and tight jeans wore their
scarves so close against their heads they looked like helmets.

He wondered whether the precise and unerring discrimination described to him by Pastor Mann at the border was
being exercised in respect of him by any of these men in the
cafe, relaxing so completely after mosque. Were any of them
curious why this Jew was wandering about Herod Gate after
midday prayers? Discomforted by this, Lev called for the bill.
The speed with which it arrived suggested that he was at the
very least being kept an eye on, but the warm smile he
received from the owner when he paid reassured him that,
if he was being watched, it was not with suspicion or alarm.

Out in the street, Lev walked against the crowds. He
thought he might visit Temple Mount but when he

approached one of the gates that led to it he was stopped by two Israeli policeman. One of them waved his index finger at him.

'No entry to the Temple Mount on Fridays.'

'Oh right. Why?'

'You Moslem?'

'No.'

'No entry to non-Moslems on Fridays.'

'When can I then?'

'Saturday to Thursday before 11a.m.'

'So if I come back here tomorrow at nine I can go through?'

'Not here.'

'Where then?'

'At Maghariba Gate at the Western Wall.'

'Only there?'

'Yes. Before eleven.'

As children, he and Udi had visited 'the site of Aravna's threshing floor' often. It had been a great adventure to them. Anyone could enter in those days and, as long as they didn't make a nuisance of themselves, they could stay as long as they liked. Lev glimpsed its wide, clear expanse through a little open door before turning away with a wave to the young policemen. Strolling back up the little lane then turning down towards Lion Gate, he could see that there was a heavy military and police presence there.

Lev went through and there before him, towering high into the sky, was the Mount of Olives. It was more built-up than he remembered, the famous olive trees less in evidence. His father's grave would be away to the right. He walked down the narrow road that led from Lion Gate to the main road. ID checking was going on down there too. The eldest of the three policemen seemed at first sight to be unnecessarily officious, but when an old Arab came to the kerb, resting heavily on a walking stick and helped by his young grandson, the policeman went out of his way to hail a cab, blowing his whistle and waving his arms about until he was successful. Not only did he help the old man into it, but he lifted the little boy in as well.

Looking east, Lev could clearly see the outline of the Jordan Mountains. It was an unusual sight. His father used to say that, as well as dust in the air, a clear view of the mountains across the Jordan Valley meant rain. Lev turned back into the Old City. He didn't want to get wet. In Jerusalem when it rained it didn't just drizzle, it sheeted down.

He heard chanting and could see a crowd walking up ahead, filling the street to such an extent that people coming in the opposite direction had to press themselves against the side walls until it had passed.

Three friars in brown habits were leading a procession of priests, monks, nuns and laity along the traditional route of Jesus to Calvary. There must have been over a hundred people altogether. Lev caught up with them outside the little Armenian church built to commemorate the place on the route where Christ had met his mother. Its doors were shut. Outside, fixed high on the wall, was a circular bronze dish. The outline of number four, in Roman numerals, was cut out of it. The three monks gathered and faced it. Restrained from entirely blocking the thoroughfare by two Israeli police officers, the crowd stopped too. In Arabic, Latin and English the three men narrated the story of the fourth Station, finishing with a quotation from Lamentations.

'All you who pass, look and see: is any sorrow like the sorrow that afflicts me.'

Meanwhile the normal clatter and racket of the bazaar continued around them. The two policemen strutted up and down between the priests and those following, keeping the street clear and talking loudly into their radios. To Lev, as he watched that afternoon, the power of the friars' message, rather than being reduced by the noise and commotion raging around them, was heightened and somehow legitimised, so concentrated was their absorption and so absolute their certainty about the importance of what they were doing. Lev admired their determination to publicly proclaim their faith whether anyone bothered to listen or not. He envied them their certainty, and wondered how it must feel not to experience indecision about the great crises of life.

At the sixth Station the friars had to compete with a music shop blaring out deafeningly loud pop music. There was no competition. The music seemed strident and insignificant beside the determination and vitality of their public witness.

They finally left the streets of the Old City after the eighth Station. Climbing a wide, gracious stairway at the back of the Church of the Holy Sepulchre, where the ninth Station was situated, the procession entered the massive church through a small door. A short dark passageway opened out into the Ethiopian orthodox chapel. The priests there looked up from their manuscripts and watched impassively as they all filed through. The three leading monks, however, returned to the streets and entered the church through the grand main door, stopping at the tenth Station in the corner of the square paved yard that led to it. Lev stayed with the ceremony until, with the fourteenth Station completed, they all stood around the huge, marble domed structure that sheltered the empty tomb of Christ. Together, they joined in remembering how the routine execution of a common criminal was transformed into the sacrifice of the Son of God by the miracle of his resurrection.

Lev went through the grand door and out into the yard, leaving the fervour behind in the dark church. He felt relieved. Nothing he had seen either in the street leading up to Herod Gate or in the Holy Sepulchre was new to him, he had witnessed it all before many times as a child, and yet now it seemed strange and exotic. The fact was, he no longer belonged here. The capacity to feel the sort of faith that was the foundation of everything he had seen this afternoon he no longer possessed; such certainty he could only aspire to.

It had turned cold and again there was rain in the air. It was almost sunset although the sun itself was lost behind the dark clouds that hung threateningly overhead.

On his way back, Lev found himself in the same lane he and Sarah had plunged down that morning. The shops were beginning to close. A group of the Hasidim were jogging, almost tumbling, down the steps towards him, joking and laughing, sidelocks swinging and white fringes peeping out from under their black jackets. Behind them was a larger, less boisterous group, and as he looked down the hill after them, he saw groups of similarly clad men. All of them, he knew, were going to the Western Wall for the start of Shabbat. Lev joined them. In the end these were his people, weren't they?

The large paved square was heaving with the ultra-ortho-dox, and brightly illuminated by huge floodlights now that daylight had faded. The atmosphere was joyous, with noth-ing of the intense fanaticism that Lev's father had brought to it and had so frightened him. No sombre reflection, none of the 'never again' bitterness on people's faces. There was a simplicity about these people's behaviour – derived, Lev was sure, from the certainty of absolute faith and the inner secu-rity that it provided. Tonight, there were groups of young people in rings, arms on each other's shoulders, dancing and singing, celebrating the good luck of being Jewish.

Yet many of the things that had scared him so much as a child were here: chests and lips pressed against the stones; worshipers rocking and stretching their necks upward; ecstatic eyes fixed firmly on the Mount high above; lips mur-muring; mouths stretched wide and gaping, loudly shouting; silent figures with heads bent in personal prayer. Through a large window of a modern building adjoining the Western Wall, Lev could see lines of young men in chairs – putative rabbis – in long black coats and black hats, yarmulkes peep-ing out from the back of their broad velvet-edged brims. They were chanting fervently from little books of scripture held reverently on their knees, rocking backwards and for-wards, their heads nodding vigorously up and down.

The area immediately in front of the Wall was so full of people pressing to reach it that it seemed there couldn't be space for any more, but still people came and were some-how absorbed, shouldering their way through. Further back, away from the dense throng, were small groups of adults chatting warmly to each other, children running amongst their legs playing hide and seek or tag. Others were talking head to head, more seriously. And further back were the young people, teenagers – the girls in short skirts and skimpy tops, the boys in oversized sweaters and white chinos – chatting, flirting and playing the fool.

Among them were other young men and women, similarly dressed but pacing here and there, singly and in pairs, with rifles slung over their shoulders. And right at the back were soldiers in more concentrated groups, watchful, talking amongst themselves and smoking cigarettes. Lev climbed the steep steps behind the soldiers that he knew would lead him up to the Jewish Quarter and, if he managed to find his way through the tangle of alleys, to the Armenian Quarter and then Damascus Gate where he could get a cab back to Sarah's. In the dark shadow of an ancient arch, he passed two Arab boys being checked over by two other boys with guns in the crooks of their arms and patterned yarmulkes pinned on the back of their heads. On the stonework above the four young cropped heads was a smeared black-stencilled image of the Kaaba in Mecca .

He paused at the top of the steps and looked back at the colossal wall. He was surprised to see the minaret beside the Al-Aqsa rising high behind it, coroneted in bright green neon. Startled, he realised that if he had been just a little higher he could have seen the domes and towers of the Holy Sepulchre as well. He knew of nowhere else where the adherents of three faiths worshiped in such close proximity. He had witnessed this unique spiritual phenomenon this afternoon. He felt enhanced, energised and privileged, yet saddened that he could share none of the ardency he had seen. Nor had he been anywhere else where religious ecstasy, idle, casual gossip, and a lively teenage 'pick-up joint' could coexist so seamlessly and with such joy, and such tolerance, as it did down there on the square.

Lev slipped back through the alleys and found Damascus Gate. Up on the main road he caught a cab back to Rehavia. This was where he would have to come to find transport for Ramallah; the drive there would be the first stage on his journey to visit Jack's brother in Nablus. It was then that it occurred to Lev that he could just as easily go back to Abou Dis and take a bus from there. If he was going to do that he'd better not tell Sarah.

* * *

The huge gold-and-cream room was crowded by the time Lev arrived. He had just come from visiting his father's grave. Sarah had gone on ahead to make sure the arrangements for the meal were in place, so he arrived alone. Looking around, he was keenly aware that he knew no one there. Some faces were vaguely familiar; some looked at him as though his was too; a few even faintly nodded at him, though none did so with enough conviction to approach him. Lev himself felt no inclination to encourage any of them with a reciprocal nod.

The cemetery had been strangely scruffy that morning. Dusty and strewn with plastic bags, it sloped steeply down the hill into the Kidron Valley opposite the Temple Mount. It was not a kind place. Unlike English cemeteries with their trees, plants and lawns, it was bleak and exposed – the souls of the dead would flee eagerly from it, without a moment's regret. Such plant-life as there was appeared to be there by accident rather than by design; the scattered vegetation was forced to break through crevices and cracks, choked in dust and rubbish. His father's simple stone box was heavily – and, it seemed to Lev, hastily – inscribed in Hebrew, and laden with pebbles. It was clear that a lot of people had been to visit Levi Dubnow's grave in the few days since the funeral. Lev added his own pebble after standing for a few minutes. He tried to think about his father as he had been when they were children, but the memory of their last meeting blotted out any happy recollections. The sun was sharply bright, flattening detail. Gentle reflection was not easy there. Eventually Lev had given up trying.

Udi caught him unawares.

'Lev. Nice to see you after all this time. When did you get in to Ben Gurion? Sarah wasn't sure.'

'I've been here a couple of days.'

'So long and no contact?'

'Sorry about that. It's taken a little time to adjust. I wanted to look around. Re-familiarise myself.'

'Naturally.'

'I didn't come through Ben Gurion as it happens; they stamp passports there.'

'And you have a British passport these days?'

'I do.'

'Ah! Our father was so proud when he first got his Israeli passport in 1949. I found it, the actual one, in his papers, just the day before yesterday.' Udi paused, putting his hands in his jacket pockets. 'Would it be such a disaster? An Israeli arrival stamp in your British passport?'

'More of an inconvenience than a disaster. Especially if I wanted to take a trip to Syria or the Lebanon while I'm here.'

'And why would one want to go to either of those two places, Lev – especially Syria?'

Unnerved by Udi's sudden presence at his shoulder, and by how quickly the edge between them had appeared, Lev attempted to regain some sort of initiative. Ignoring Udi's final question, he stepped forward and embraced his brother, brushing his lips on his cheeks three times.

'Nice to see you too, Udi.'

Lev heard the faint ring of sarcasm that he hadn't meant. His use of the word 'too' had been unfortunate and careless, and he regretted it. He took a step back and looked at his brother. Udi was smiling at him in a way that Lev remembered only too clearly. It still had the power to disturb him. He looked quickly away.

When Lev had tried to describe that smile in the past he had resorted to using clumsy phrases like 'demeaning levity' or adjectives like 'dismissive' or 'ironic'. However as he gazed at his brother today, after so many years, he saw to his surprise that accompanying Udi's usual bolt-on smile there was in his brother's eyes what he would describe to Sarah later as 'a sort of defensive uncertainty'.

Udi had worn glasses since his early twenties. The lenses he was now wearing were much thicker than they had been then. As a consequence, the look that Lev recollected so well was now more prominent than ever, yet more difficult to accurately identify. 'Defensive uncertainty' was a guess.

When Lev left Israel, Udi had been the taller of the two, as he had been since their early teens. It had meant that Lev always had to raise his eyes to meet his. As a youngster, Lev had read into this discrepancy a metaphor for their relationship – or rather a metaphor for how his father in particular expected him to regard Udi. He was briefly pleased to find that their eyes were now level. He hadn't grown, so Udi must have shrunk. These things happen as you grow older.

Otherwise his brother looked well, though substantially heavier. Darker skinned too. He had always been the darkest of the three of them – the 'Arab' of the family – but his face, and his neck against the sharp white of his shirt, seemed more deeply tanned than ever, even cultivatedly so.

'Been away?'

'I was in Eilat when the news came through.'

'Ah.'

His hair was still jet black with no hint of grey. He wore it in a style that would have needed frequent attention, parted to the left and crisply sheared around the ears. A tailored black suit masked his burgeoning girth. His shoulders were broad, his back straight, just as their father's had always been. He wore his clothes well despite his increased weight, presenting a compact figure – strong without being particularly powerful.

What Lev had forgotten was how close Udi stood to those to whom he talked. When they were young Lev had found this habit intimidating, as if Udi was deliberately imposing his authority, even superiority, over him. In the most difficult times, Lev had believed Udi was actually intending to be threatening. Instinctively Lev took a step back, and looked away across the long, cavernous room which was the Menachem Begin Salon.

'Very posh, this place.'

It shimmered. There were three enormous and very ornate chandeliers. Along one of the heavily-draped walls were six pairs of sparkling French windows with gilt and white frames; along another, three pairs of marble pillars. The floor was highly polished parquet.

'You don't approve?'

'No it's fine. Very splendid. Entirely tasteless, but very grand. Very grand indeed.'

'The Begin Salons – there are two of them here – are supposed to be identical to two interlocking ballrooms somewhere in St Petersburg.'

'Appropriate then.'

'I thought so.'

'There's quite a mob in here, Udi. Wasn't the other one available?'

'Excessive to have hired two, don't you think?'

'Of course, far too excessive.'

Lev had tried hard to keep any hint of sarcasm out of his tone. Again he hadn't succeeded.

'Especially as we decided to provide a small meal.'

'I wondered about that.'

'Leah thought it was appropriate.'

'So Sarah said.'

They stood silently.

'I was very sorry to hear about you and your Joanna.'

'Really.'

'Really. Such things … Well you must have been very disappointed.'

'"Such things", as I think you were about say – banal as it is to say – do happen.'

'Not often, here, to be truthful. Not in the society we've built.'

'Oh really. There must be a lot of unhappy couples here then.'

Lev was tempted to mention Bruno and Sarah but resisted.

'No. I think that's quite a harsh and uninformed judgment. For a start we believe in relationships, and in working hard at them, despite the difficulties that inevitably occur.'

'Implying?'

'Implying nothing, Lev. It is just that we regard marriage – any relationship – as important to preserve. A gift – a sacrament, as the Christians would say. Not something to be entered into lightly or dissolved easily.'

'Do you think Joanna and I approached our relationship any differently?'

'I'm sure you didn't. Well I'm sure *you* didn't. As for your Joanna, I'm not so sure. You gave up a great deal for her. From where I stood at the time it didn't seem she was giving up very much for you at all. It was all a bit of an adventure for her. At least that's how it seemed to us.'

'Us?'

'Our father and me. And Sarah too if it comes to that. It was always going to be difficult for you two.'

'It was?'

'That much was always clear. She was such an abrasive person. Don't you think? Now? Looking back? Now that it's all over finally.'

'No I don't. Not even now. Joanna was bright, quick and questioning. She wanted to know about everything, however insignificant. I can certainly see how a woman with such insatiable curiosity might appear a challenge to people in a society like this. It certainly appeared that she was a complete anathema to you and Dad. You both made that very clear at the time.'

'That may be overstating it just a little. One of your rather irritating little habits, exaggeration, which it seems you have not shed in the intervening years. That she was a challenge, I would concede.'

'I can see you've lost none of your condescending pomposity in the intervening years, either, Udi. And for sure she found it very difficult to subscribe to some of those tiresome aphorisms that Dad used so often when we were children.'

Lev smiled.

'I remember one time in particular.'

'And what was that?'

'You'll be sure to remember it, Udi. Jo had never heard it before although it wasn't particularly original.'

'Our father said many things. Which one did your Joanna take such exception to?'

'You know, I can actually remember the precise moment when he said it to her. She almost burst with indignation. Would have, if she'd realised he was actually quite serious.'

'Don't keep me on tenterhooks Lev … I've obviously missed something. I can't recollect our father saying anything that wasn't wise and – what's more – correct and true.'

'I would have said closed and insular.'

'But that's you, Lev. You always were attracted to disorder, rather than order and the discipline necessary to achieve it. That approach hasn't brought you much happiness or contentment, it appears. Has it Lev?'

'You know nothing about my life, Udi.'

'Your failure with your Joanna is a clear indication, I would have thought.'

'You know nothing about what happened between us.'

'No doubt you will tell us all about it at some stage before you leave. Now, are you going to let me in on this particular example of one of our father's "aphorisms", as you like to call them, or are you going to keep me guessing? I would like to see whether or not I can finally share something with your ex-partner. I failed to share very much with her when I knew her.'

'Your loss, Udi, your loss. Anyway, Dad and Joanna were sitting at breakfast in the conservatory. Jo was asking him why Jews brushed the mezuzah with the tips of their fingers and then touched their lips every time they went in and out of their houses. He was on his most patronizingly patient best behaviour. "Not only their houses Joanna, not only the front door of their houses". "But why, Mr Dubnow, why?" He probably couldn't remember why. So rather than admit it, he sententiously blustered, "If you are going to spend any time in this country, young lady, you should try as far as you can to adhere to the principle that fathers here try hard to instil in their children. If your father tells you to jump, Miss Payne, you reply, 'how high?' Not 'why?'" You'd have thought he was quoting from Solomon himself rather than churning out a hackneyed old saying that thousands had churned out before him.'

Udi chuckled. 'I can see how that would not have appealed to your Joanna. You must see, even from that rather amusing little story, that you two were quite unsuited for anything long term. You were so different. The two of you came from such different backgrounds, cultures—'

'You mean she was a goy?'

'Goy. Gentile. These are just words Lev.'

'Words are very important. It was because of the words you and Dad used that I left.'

'Lev, let's not kid ourselves. You would have left whatever had been said.'

'That isn't true.'

'Isn't it? The point is, she wasn't a Jew. That was the important thing. It would have had implications for the future, for any children you may have had. Praise God you didn't.'

'Jo lost a son in childbirth.'

Udi went pale.

'Lev, I didn't know. I wouldn't have …'

'There's no reason for you to have known. No one knew except close family—' Lev bit his tongue. '*Joanna's* family. And other close friends in London. That's what I meant.'

Udi had perceptibly winced at Lev's dismissal of his own family, but there was also a hint of something else in his eyes.

Lev wondered what Udi was thinking – that Joanna and he had brought the loss of their child on themselves? Was he really that pious?

They stood silently. Udi recovered first.

'You've had a very unhappy time, Lev. And now our father.'

'I don't want to distress you even more than I think I have already, but Dad's dying is the least of it.'

'Then why have you come?'

'For you and Sarah of course. Now he's gone, I thought it might just be possible to re-establish some sort of relationship with you. And I am a Jew, Udi. It is appropriate for me to be at such an occasion, at the side of my brother and sister.'

'Yes, of course it is. I thought so too, on reflection. And I should say how grateful we are that you have come.'

'I wasn't looking for your gratitude. It seems to separate

the two of you from me.'

'That's how it is though, Lev, how can it be any other way? It was you that chose to leave. Sarah and I have been through a great deal together since then. Neither of us has children. Then there were our father's strokes and finally his death. You have not been here to share it with us.'

'And Bruno and Sarah splitting up?'

'Yes, there was that too. Although that particular squalid little episode could have been avoided. I'm afraid I had little patience with either of them; they were both very foolish, and much too hasty. If they had just given themselves a little time I'm sure they could have accommodated each other.'

'Lived separate lives, you mean. Had affairs on the side. Is that how you and Leah manage?'

Udi ignored Lev's question.

'I'm sorry Udi, that was impertinent.'

Udi shrugged and looked away. For a second he looked sad, but again it was he who regrouped and restarted the conversation.

'Sarah has probably told you about our plans for Dad's house?'

'You mean *your* plans.'

'You have reservations?'

'I have, yes.'

'You have … I see.'

Udi took a step back, plainly irritated. He looked away again across the crowded room, his right foot tapping impatiently on the polished floor.

'I have no intention of claiming a share of any proceeds, but—'

'You haven't? Why not?'

'I have enough Udi, and since it was me that abandoned you all—'

'Your words, not mine.'

'But that doesn't prevent me having a view about the rights and wrongs of what you are proposing for the disposal of the house.' Lev took a deep breath. 'I think it was quite shocking that you had the house redecorated for valuation before Dad was even dead. Who paid for the work to be done?'

'Family funds.'

'You mean Dad's funds.'

'He kept a separate account for maintenance work on the house, although he didn't make much use of it during the last few years. You will remember he was always very prudent with money – was until the day he died. He gave Sarah access to the account when he went into hospital.'

'I don't suppose she told him you were planning to buy it.'

'The conservatory needed repair; Dad knew that. We didn't want to bother him with the rest of it.'

'I bet you didn't. All that said, Udi, what I'm quite sure of is that you will offer a fair price. I'm quite sure also that you and Leah will eventually need the space.' Udi shot his brother a sharp glance. Lev tried not to look away. 'However, I also think you should put the old place on the open market, see what it actually fetches. I don't think what you are proposing is the way the thing should be done and I know that Sarah is anxious about it. By all means top the highest bidder, you can't be short Udi, but see what it manages to fetch first.'

'What's this about Sarah? She seemed to agree pretty readily when I said I wanted to buy the property.'

'Of course she did, Udi. It's how she is. I sometimes think the expression "go with the flow" originated with Sarah. See it from her point of view. She's lost one brother over a family dispute so she's hardly going to risk falling out with the other. Since she's never going to say anything to you about it, I am. On her behalf, if you like.'

'I see.'

'I hope you do, because I'm quite determined.'

On cue, Udi took a step forward.

'You know Lev ...'

'What Udi?'

'You know you've really got quite a nerve, coming back here after all this time and laying down the law like this about what I should or should not do about our father's house – a house, may I remind you, you were once only too anxious to see the back of. Pretending to be representing Sarah against me. Attempting to divide us. What right do you think you have?'

'I am still a member of the family.'

'Oh no you're not. You forfeited a place in this family by running off with that woman. When Sarah told me of your intention to attend this function, it was against my better judgment to permit you.'

'Permit me?'

'Yes Lev, *permit* you. Dad wouldn't have wanted you here, I can tell you that. You defied him, deserted us, gave up your faith and ratted on Israel. And for what? For so little. A ridiculous and rather unpleasant woman, who never let any opportunity go by to deride our values, our religion and traditions and the efforts we were making to fashion a life for ourselves here. You were so hell-bent on getting your hands on her, weren't you? Any concern for the inevitable consequences to us, your family, was disregarded completely. We warned you it would bring you unhappiness. And it has, hasn't it? Twice over. Did you take any notice of us, our cries of protest, of outrage, at what you were embarking on? No Lev. You didn't. And now look where you are. A relationship in ruins. Your illegitimate child dead. It was so predictable that it would turn out badly. Just desserts Lev. Just desserts.'

Lev gasped at the force and bitterness of his brother's assault.

'You have no real place here anymore,' he continued. 'You don't belong. You are here under sufferance – as a spectator, no more and no less. Realise that, behave accordingly and then leave.'

Lev took a deep breath.

'You are a bully, Udi. You are pious and overbearing, and apparently quite cruel now, as well. I'll leave Jerusalem when I'm good and ready.' He looked at his brother directly, as he had never done before. 'You are a bully, just as you always have been. Sarah and I have always given way. But we're not children anymore. I certainly won't give way to you over the house, and I'll do my best to see Sarah doesn't either.'

'Is everything alright between you two? What's happened?'

Lev had not seen Sarah since arriving, but suddenly she was there between them, looking anxiously from one to the other. She had been gnawing at her lower lip, Lev could see.

'Fine, little sister, fine. Everything's OK. Where have you been? You must be very busy.'

'There's a lot to do, Lev. There are so many people here to pay their respects. You two should be circulating. That's what's expected, you know. Leah's done sterling work with the caterers, Udi. Everything looks perfect. When do you think we should call everyone through to eat?'

'Give everyone a little more time, Sarah. Lots of Dad's old friends won't have seen each other for some time.'

'I've some good news for you little sister.'

'You have?'

'Udi has just agreed to put Dad's house on the open market. That's what we were talking over. Now, isn't that good news?'

She brightened and turned to her older brother with a grin.

'I'm so glad Udi. Thanks so much. Good old Lev, eh? He only needs to turn up and everything seems to get sorted out. Thanks so much, Udi. I can't tell you how relieved I am. It's so much more straightforward this way.'

She kissed Udi gently on the cheek and he hugged her. Lev could see that Sarah's gratitude had placated him. Stepping back to observe them, Lev was struck by their unselfconscious affection for each other. It was so effortless. With Joanna, he had experienced something like this for the first time in his life: an easy affection based on complete trust and mutual regard; a willingness to listen, to support and, when necessary, to protect and defend.

Lev wished he understood why his relationship with his brother remained so difficult. It was not just because of the fracture over Joanna, or because he had deserted. He watched his sister and brother talking head to head about the arrangements for the day. Had he really expected it to be any different after all this time, as if their separation would somehow have closed the divide? Lev felt excluded.

The relationship Udi and Sarah had was closer than anything he could hope for with either of them.

He knew that the conversation he'd just had with Udi couldn't have happened had they not been brothers, with a shared history and a shared childhood. Certain things between them were immutable and couldn't be changed by words alone, however bitter and extreme. And yet that same shared childhood had gifted Udi and Sarah the gentle, affectionate sympathy they plainly had for each other. Why didn't she resent Udi's casual assumption of authority? What was it she had said yesterday? 'He'd just like to live in our old family house. I understand that, Lev. He's very sentimental, you know, underneath. '

Udi was now handshaking his way from person to person. He did it well, affably: a few quiet words here, a smile and a hug there. At school, Lev had always been in his brother's shadow. Udi had been so well-behaved, so courteous and respectful to his superiors, so clever and correct. 'Exemplary' and 'Excellent' appeared all the time on his end-of-term reports. It wasn't that Lev hadn't done well himself, but Udi was always just a little ahead of him in everything. A teacher had even once said to Lev, 'I would never have guessed that you were Udi Dubnow's brother.' What a thing to say to a child! And how often had his father said, 'I don't know why you can't be more like Udi?'

Udi was talking now to an elderly man with a thick, white moustache.

'One of Dad's old cronies from the IDF,' said Sarah. 'They were in the Sinai together and then up on the Golan. I'd better speak to him. I'll be back in a minute.'

She seemed to know the old man very well and she was

soon hugging and kissing him. To Lev, his face wasn't familiar at all.

Lev went out through the French windows for a smoke and found himself on a terrace overlooking a garden with a meticulously tended stretch of lawn surrounded by beds of white and light blue flowers.

'Lev Dubnow? No, I'm sure that's who you are.'

It was his Auntie Golda, his mother's younger sister – very old now, and defiantly sturdy.

'It is you, isn't it, Lev?'

She leant heavily on a walking stick, her head belligerently preceding her shoulders. The severe look in her eye didn't invite interruption.

'So you've come home at last, have you? Well you're a bit late, if you ask me, young man. I'm not going to say I'm pleased to see you, because I'm not. As far as I am concerned you might as well have put a pistol to your dear father's head the day you left. It would have been far more merciful. It was you who killed him, Lev Dubnow, not the stroke. You broke the spirit of a good man who should have enjoyed a long and happy old age. You are not worthy to bear his name. Such a very good man. That such a man should have had such a son as you.'

Lev opened his mouth to say something.

'Don't, Lev. There's nothing you can say to me that I'll want to hear. I'm an old woman now. I don't have to listen to anyone anymore if I don't care to, and I certainly don't care to hear anything you have to say. Go back to London or wherever it is you live. Sooner the better as far as I'm concerned.'

She looked hard at him, her head nodding violently

from side to side, then turned away, red-faced and trembling, and went back inside.

Lev was shaken.

Was that what the family thought? And was it true? If Udi had left, perhaps. But Lev? Hardly. He sighed.

'Having a hard time, Lev Dubnow? Or is it Lev Payne these days?'

'No it's not. Why anyone should think I took on Joanna's name, I don't know. I'm sorry, do I know you?'

'Rachel Sahed. I'm an old friend of Sarah's. Hi.'

She put her hand out in a very straightforward manner and shook his with a firm grip. Rachel was tall with strong wide hips that looked good in her tailored skirt. Everything about her was strong and athletic. Her face had no excess flesh, even under her chin; her cheekbones were prominent yet graceful, and her brown eyes were large, frank, and radiant with good health. Her hair, auburn-and-blonde streaked, curled inward against her neck at shoulder length.

'Sorry. Sarah mentioned you the other day but we haven't met, have we?'

'Long time ago. When I was but a little girl and you were a scrummy young doctor.' She grinned.

'Perhaps you can me tell why I am supposed to have changed my name to Payne?'

'Because you are one?'

Lev looked puzzled.

'Joke. *Pain*, you know – P-A-I-N.'

'Seriously, why should anyone think I would have changed my surname to Jo's? You know who Joanna is, I take it?'

'I certainly do. How could I not? The Dubnow family has seemed at times to have been completely obsessed by her. I think the family thought you were ashamed of them – and ashamed of Israel, if it comes to that. They thought you'd try to distance yourself from them all once you settled in London, that you might try to shed your Jewishness. Changing your surname would have been a very predictable first step.'

'Frankly, it never occurred to me. And as far as being ashamed of Israel is concerned, I've tried not to give much thought to what you all now call "the Palestinian problem". In my day we didn't use the word "Palestinian". Golda Meir refused to use it, did you know that? Joanna went on about how awfully Israel was behaving from time to time, of course, but that was just how she was – indignant, outraged by all sorts of things. Unless the situation here was brought up specifically I tried not to think much about it.'

'So how did you deal with us? When we were brought up?'

'Shrug my shoulders and smile disarmingly?'

'Was that good enough?'

'No, but when I left here all those years ago it wasn't much of an issue for me, and it wasn't much of an issue for people in England, either. I have to say though my views on it all have changed some since I arrived. I hadn't expected to see what I've seen – and I've only been here a couple of days, and not more than a mile or so from Rehavia.'

'Surely a son of Levi Dubnow isn't developing a conscience about Israel?'

'A couple of episodes I witnessed yesterday I found really rather troubling.'

'I see.'

'If that upsets you, I'm sorry.'

'It doesn't.'

'Well I've upset Sarah, I know I have. The thing is, she's too close to it all, too used to it. I suspect you all are. I've seen more hatred in the eyes of people in the last few days than I ever did before I left. Perhaps I was just unaware. Perhaps I just didn't know enough Arabs.'

He lit another cigarette.

'Udi has just called me a spectator.'

'I can understand why he might say that,' said Rachel.

'Well I don't much like the word. It implies that what I am seeing isn't really anything to do with me and that I'm getting some sort of prurient, vicarious excitement out of looking in at it; as if I want to go back home and regale my dinner party guests with gruesome stories, demonstrating what a good and aware Jew I've become. What I've seen up until now hasn't excited me, it has deeply saddened me. And the experience hasn't felt vicarious either. I'm part of what's going on here; I can't escape it.'

'I think you're right.'

'I am what I am. And I happen to be a Jew. The Jews are my people. The trouble is that I'd like to think my people are the good guys but, from what I've seen so far, they are not behaving like the good guys, they're really not. I have seen nice, very nice, ordinary people stand around as if nothing untoward was happening, when something very cruel and very ugly was taking place right beside them. My sister, my own little sister, watched with me a public spectacle, a hideous drama played out between children, and then justified it in the same terms I had used to describe how awful it was! When the abnormal becomes normal in society, as well as in human relations, then you are in real trouble. As a doctor I treat patients who behave abnormally everyday. If I were Israel's doctor I would probably order that it be restrained for its own good.'

Lev shrugged his shoulders and smiled at her.

'Sorry for the rant. I'm not sounding like me.'

'Don't be sorry. It was good to hear a son of Dubnow talking sense for a change. Thanks Lev, thanks for the conversation.'

'What?'

He looked at her in surprise.

'I wasn't aware you smoked, Lev.'

'Do you always have to creep up behind me like some sort of assassin, Udi? Contrary to what you probably think, I have very few vices. I hardly drink, I masturbate rarely and I puff weed not all; but I do smoke Virginia tobacco, and fine Turkish when I can get hold of it, as well. Too much for my own health possibly and I'll probably die regretting it but yes, Udi, I do smoke, I'm afraid. I'll put it out at once, if it offends you.'

Snorting with laughter, Rachel excused herself.

'Don't show off, Lev. I didn't know you'd become vulgar as well as everything else.'

'Everything else? What do you mean everything else?'

'You've spent the last two days distressing Sarah with your outbursts of self-righteousness, and now this afternoon you seem to have quite gratuitously upset Auntie Golda as well.'

'I'm sorry. I really don't want to upset anyone, you least of all.'

'There was one other thing I wanted to talk to you about.'

'Yes? And that was?'

'You knew Dad was ill some time ago didn't you?'

'I did, yes. How do you know that?'

'Just putting two and two together.'

'And getting five no doubt! Yes, Sarah has been writing to me.'

'She didn't tell me. Did she write often?'

'Once or twice a year.'

'I see.'

'Don't be angry with her. It is what brothers and sisters do. I regret very much not writing to you, actually.'

'Really?'

'Really. I should have.'

'Be that as it may, Lev, you didn't, did you? Anyway, since you were so well informed about everything that was happening here, why didn't you feel inclined to come back and see Dad before he died?'

'And distress him more than he was already?'

'But you and Joanna had broken up before he became ill, hadn't you?'

'We had.'

'Well?'

'You mean that would have been my ticket back into his good books? I hope you don't think that he would have been pleased that Joanna and I had broken up.'

'No I don't think that for one minute.'

'I hope not.'

'But wasn't that why you didn't come back here before he died?'

'What? Do you think I was ashamed to come back, is that it? That I didn't want Dad to know that it had all gone wrong. I wouldn't have cared a damn whether he'd known or not.'

'You asked Sarah not to tell anyone, apparently.'

'It was my business. It was hard enough to bear on its own, without having to deal with the possibility of condescending overtures from here as well. I didn't come back because too much had happened between Dad and me. He would not have been fooled by feeble placatory words, and frankly I wasn't prepared to try and placate him.'

'I was not thinking in terms of placation. I was thinking that perhaps you could have asked him for his forgiveness.'

'Let me tell you this very clearly. I am not a prodigal son. I repent nothing. I could have said I was sorry, but it wouldn't have been sincere. Dad would have realised that. He may have been an unpleasant and vengeful old man but he wasn't a fool. And there's something else too. You may not know this, because there seems to be quite a lot you don't know, Udi. He came to London. Yes, Dad actually visited London. He was a member of some sort of discreet delegation on behalf of his mates in the government. He came to London, and he never made any attempt to find me.'

'If he was doing some sensitive work for the government, as you say, he couldn't just break off to go and have a cup of tea with just anyone as the fancy took him. He obviously had important work to do.'

'Maybe, maybe, but if he had really wanted to he could have, you know that. To find an NHS doctor in London is not difficult with a bit of persistence. Anyway, I wasn't just anyone – I was his son. You told me earlier that I had forfeited my rights in the family by deserting you all and going to live in London. Well, however unreasonable this may sound, Dad finally forfeited any vestiges of affection I had left in me when I discovered he had been within a mile or two of my hospital and had not even slipped into a phone box to enquire whether I, his son – his son, Udi – was on duty.'

'I see.'

'Our father had a chance to repair some of the damage and he didn't take it. I tell you this, if I'd known he was there at the time, I would have gone and looked for him. He didn't take the chance when it arose, and by not doing so he just piled on more damage. Just like you've done today Udi. I came here to attempt to lay a foundation for the future, so that perhaps Sarah might take a trip occasionally without incurring your displeasure. I even hoped that you might come to London and see your little brother. Don't you understand, Udi? I didn't come to fight or argue with you. I came to be with you both, my brother and my sister, to share your grief.'

Udi looked uncomfortable, restive.

'For God's sake, Udi …'

'How interesting you should use such a phrase.'

'What are you talking about now?'

'In Europe and the US God's name is only ever invoked in moments of exasperation and anger. Here of course we only invoke his name to praise him, to thank him or to ask for his assistance.'

Udi glanced sharply at his brother.

'I hear from Sarah that you are thinking of taking a trip into the Territories.'

'I am.'

'I should think you'll be very welcome there given the views you now appear to hold. Certainly more welcome than you are here.'

Udi turned on his heel and went back in.

## 3. Beyond Qalandia

'There's dust in the air again.'

'Is that right?'

Sarah bustled into the kitchen, without looking Lev in the eye.

'Do you want some coffee?'

'Yes thanks. That's kind.'

She was, it seemed to Lev, being very busy, determinedly so, head down, spooning out the instant coffee from the jar in her hand with excessive deliberation.

'Sarah?'

'Yes?'

The tone of her voice was flat, dull; it lacked warmth.

'Is anything up? Is there anything wrong?'

She carefully poured the milk into each cup.

'Fine time to go to Ramallah.'

'What?'

'The news. You must have heard the news?'

'I have yes.'

'Well?'

'What about it?'

'There's been trouble there.'

'Five dead including a nine year old, a three- or four-storey house completely demolished, and you call it "trouble"?'

'Whatever's happened has happened.'

'Five people died. That's what happened.'

'There's not very much we can do about that, is there?'

'Not now they're dead, no, but we could feel a little sadness, couldn't we, give a few moments thought to those left grieving; even perhaps protest?'

'You protest if you like, I've got my life to get on with.'

Sarah brought Lev's coffee through and gave it to him.

'Thanks.'

'What I'm getting at, Lev, is that it'll be more dangerous than ever for a Jew to go anywhere near Ramallah. At least for the next few days.'

'You want me to delay my trip, is that it?'

'It'll be dangerous, Lev, please say you're not going to Ramallah, today of all days?'

'I'm afraid I am, Sarah. The way things are here, something else will only happen next week and then something else the week after. There'll always be some reason to put off going. So if I'm going at all – and I am – I might as well go today as any other day.'

'At the very least avoid Ramallah. You could go straight to Nablus. You can probably get a cab straight to the Za'tara intersection, or even all the way to Hawara, if you ask around at Damascus Gate. Please, Lev. Splash out. Take a cab to Hawara.' She stopped talking suddenly and looked anxious. 'No, that's probably not possible, not these days.'

'Why?'

'None of the drivers will have the permits.'

'Why?'

'Arabs aren't allowed to go to other parts of the West Bank anymore. They have to stay near where they live, unless they've got permits of course. I don't know what the rules are exactly.'

'I shouldn't think that was very good for business, would you? If you were an Arab cabbie.'

'That's their look-out. Why don't you just stay here and use my flat as your base, taking little trips here and there as you have been doing. You had a nice time in Hebron the other day didn't you? You enjoyed Haifa.'

'Haifa's much further away than Nablus.'

'No it's not, it only took you a couple of hours on the bus to Haifa.'

'But it'll take me much less time to get to Nablus, that's why I'm taking in Ramallah on the way.'

'But it won't, Lev. It'll take you all day, perhaps longer.'

'But Udi and I used to drive up to Nablus when we were students to get soap for mum. We would get back by lunchtime and that was in Udi's old Morris.'

'That's a long time ago Lev. There are checkpoints these days, queues, delays. You don't understand what it's like now. You might even get turned back. The soldiers might not let you through; might not let you anywhere near Ramallah. Especially after last night's little fracas.'

'There you go again.'

'What?'

'You just don't see it do you Sarah?'

He shrugged his shoulders.

'I need a smoke. I'll go out on to the balcony if you don't mind. The coffee's great. Thanks.'

A few minutes later Sarah came out to join him wrapped up tight against the morning air in her old dressing gown. She was clutching a cup in one hand and a slice of toast in the other, distractedly tearing pieces off with her teeth. She threw the last scrap over the balcony and a small bird that looked to Lev like a sparrow pounced on it as it hit the ground. After staring distastefully down at her coffee she put the half empty cup down on the windowsill.

'Why have you got to go and see this man anyway?'

'You know why. I've told you a thousand times. I promised.'

'But you hardly know him.'

'Who?'

'This Jack that you've taken such a shine to.'

'A promise is a promise, and anyway I want to see something more of the Territories before I go home.'

'I can't think why. Sometimes I think we should give all that land back to the Arabs, close the borders and let them get on with it and to hell with the lot of them. Those cranks in the settlements can stay put for all I care, if that's what they want to do. If they don't like it then they can come back here and live with the rest of us can't they? That's what Rachel's always saying should happen anyway.'

'Does she really?'

'Something like that.'

'You do mean Rachel Sahed?'

'Yes of course. Why is it so important what Rachel says?'

'It's not especially.'

'I don't listen to her half the time.'

Sarah put her hands on her hips.

'I suppose you'll do just exactly what you want to do, like you've always done, despite what I say. You've not changed, Lev, have you? I suppose that's just how you are; awkward and stubborn. Be careful, that's all. I haven't been beyond

Qalandia for years; people say it's very dangerous these days.'

She cuddled herself, arms across her chest, her hands cupping each elbow. Lev went across to her and put his arms around her hunched shoulders.

'And isn't that a pity? As students, Udi and I used to have great times in Ramallah, and I remember Dad taking you to Nablus so you could draw in the Old City.'

'I remember that too. It was for my school project at the end of my third year. It was so different then. I wonder how many of those lovely old buildings are still intact now. There's been such a lot of trouble there over the years.'

'There's that word again.'

'I don't follow.'

'"Trouble". Is that how you all manage to deal with things? By using words like 'trouble'. And what was that word you used a minute ago? "Fracas", that was it.'

'They're just words Lev.'

'I take words seriously these days.'

'I should think that's Joanna's doing. It sounds just like something she would say.'

'I expect you're right.'

'I could have said, "There's been a great deal of fighting there over the years." Would that have made you feel better?'

'It would have been more honest. Words are important, Sarah. They used to diminish what was going on in Northern Ireland by calling it "The Troubles", when what was actually going on was a civil war, and it seems it's much the same here. "Trouble" is rowdiness after a soccer match or a group of blokes getting plastered on a Saturday night and kicking in a few shop windows, not five innocent people slaughtered and their house reduced to a shell.'

'You don't know that.'

'What, that five people died in Ramallah last night?'

'No, that their house was reduced to a shell.'

'No I don't. And do you know why?'

'I'm sure you're about to tell me.'

'Because the newspapers here never describe what is actually happening.'

'I'd rather not know.'

'But if they did? If individual deaths and injuries were accurately reported, who knows, you may in the end feel so weary of reading about fighting and killing that you would actively campaign against it to try and stop it. That happened in the US over Vietnam, didn't it? Words matter a lot.'

He grimaced sadly.

'That is exactly what Jo used to say, as it happens. As far as Nablus is concerned, and what is or is not left of it, I'll be able to see for myself tomorrow, won't I?'

'You will be careful though won't you, Lev?'

'Don't worry so much. I will be careful, Sarah, I promise.'

'So what route are you going to take?'

'A minibus from Damascus Gate to Qalandia, then on to Ramallah. I'll mooch around for a few hours and then get another minibus to Nablus. Probably stay there tonight, unless I get held up.'

'Just don't get held up! Please don't spend the night in Ramallah. That would be asking for trouble!'

'Don't worry. There's no reason for me to get held up in Ramallah is there? Tomorrow after breakfast I plan to try and find Waseem's village. According to my map it's some-where between Nablus and Tulkarem.'

'But it'll all be so dangerous.'

'I'll be alright, Sarah. Don't worry.'

He gave her another quick hug.

'Are you going to give me a lift to Damascus Gate? I can easily walk if you don't fancy it.'

'No. Of course I'll take you.'

'And I expect you'll want some soap?'

'To visit Nablus and not buy soap? Unthinkable!'

\* \* \*

Sarah dropped him across the street from where the minibuses were parked. He walked across towards them as she drove away.

'Hebron? Bethlehem?'

'No. Abou Dis.'

'Abou Dis?'

'Yes.'

'Herod Gate.'

'Ah right. Thanks.'

He looked round to see where Sarah had got to and when he was sure she was gone he walked away from Damascus Gate along the outside of the city walls towards Herod. There were a few traders out along the pavement but nothing like as many as there were on Fridays.

'Abou Dis?'

'You want to go to Abou Dis?'

'I do.'

'That bus there.'

Because all the other passengers were women, Lev had to squash himself in on the back seat with four other men. Only a fragile looking fold-down seat at the front was still vacant; an elderly man with a heavily wrinkled face heaved himself aboard and sat down on it with a thud. His advanced age made that acceptable.

He was dressed in a crisp red and white hata and a jalabia, with an old-fashioned double-breasted jacket. He showed his ID to the driver, who waved it away impatiently. The old man shook his head in bewilderment; he had probably been required to show his identification papers to so many different officials during so many different periods of government that, rather than make a mistake, he produced them now for anybody who seemed to be in a position of authority.

It appeared though as if it all mattered very little to him; his eyes had such a distant, absent expression. Perhaps it was the look that some old people have which betrays a mind that is elsewhere, a mind that is reviewing, recollecting and ordering, trying to make sense of a long life. Or perhaps it was simply the expression of an old man inwardly at prayer, mentally reciting lines from the Koran or prayers from his youth. In either case, with one foot already in paradise, the old gentleman's present circumstances, as he sat on the fragile seat, waiting to be taken to Abou Dis, were, it seemed, an irrelevance.

It occurred to Lev that he had seen a lot of people in and around Jerusalem over the last couple of weeks who, irrespective of their physical circumstances, were clearly elsewhere in their heads. These people, Jews and Arabs of all ages, ordinary in all other aspects, didn't need the serenity of a mosque or a synagogue to be in touch with God; they could be walking in the street, sitting surrounded by the babble of friends and relatives, or sipping a coffee in the sun. Sometimes their heads would be nodding gently to the rhythm of the lines they were privately reciting; sometimes their lips might be fractionally moving; nevertheless, they would be plainly out of touch with their surroundings and the passing of time. He and Joanna had seen sanyasi in India who had behaved similarly, but they were special people, accorded respect and space by those around them. In Jerusalem it seemed to Lev that the capacity to lose touch with the physical world while being completely immersed in it went generally unremarked, and was not just reserved for a special few.

It seemed to be the custom for passengers to pay for the trip during the journey. Over shoulders, from hand to hand, each of them sent their money forward to the driver. The fare was two shekels but as Lev only had a five shekel piece he passed that to the woman in front of him. Two or three minutes later, to Lev's surprise, his change was passed to him. Since no one had looked back at him during the whole transaction, he wondered who had made the calculation and how he had been identified as the only passenger who required change.

After ten or fifteen minutes, the jumble of concrete blocks he had been forced to climb over on the evening of his arrival appeared ahead.

\* \* \*

The barrier at Abou Dis was two to three metres high, entirely blocking the street and splitting the village in two. It looked like a mound of rubble haphazardly dumped, but at its core were slim concrete slabs set on splayed plinths. If the ground had been flat they would have formed a barrier penetrable only by the young and strong, or with the assistance of ramps and rubble-piles. But because the ground hadn't been entirely flattened there were triangular gaps where the splayed plinths tilted away from the vertical. It was through one of these that Lev had climbed a few nights before. As he approached, he could see that particular gap had been sealed with barbed wire. There was a jeep parked opposite, with soldiers sitting inside ensuring the wire stayed in place.

Judging by the number of people still coming and going, and the number of shops, mostly boarded up, the cross-roads must once have been very busy. It was probably on one of the main thoroughfares linking Jerusalem to the Jordan Valley, winding its way from the slopes and hillsides of Judea; in Solomon's time, possibly a caravan route, or even a path for shepherds and their flocks going to Jerusalem to sell cheese and skins.

Lev followed the crowd up towards a mosque, looking for a suitable breach in the barrier. Children slipped easily through the smaller gaps; where the gaps were slightly wider, young people with flexible bodies, did the same. There were twisted steel loops on the top of each slab, designed for a crane hook. The tarmac surface of the road was torn up and rough, evidence that heavy cranes on caterpillar tracks had been used to swing each piece of the barrier into place. The loops were now utilised to hang bags so that people could squeeze through unencumbered, or as handgrips for those with enough strength to heave themselves over. Further up past the mosque was the new main crossing point. It looked as though one slab had been levered up to create a gap just wide enough for most people to get through. A rock had been forced under the plinth to hold it in place. Even so a rubble stairway had had to be constructed, because the gap was still a metre or so above the ground.

Lev stood watching for a few minutes.

Babies tightly swaddled in shawls were passed from hand to hand, large bundles and oversize bags likewise. To Lev, standing there watching the third or fourth baby being lifted up, through the gap, then down the other side, the bright colours of their shawls seemed a statement of their parents' defiance. Practically, the shawls should have been grey, black or brown. The baby being passed down at that moment, from unknown hand to unknown hand, was wrapped in a shawl of lemon yellow, and it had smears of dust and dirt on it. Indeed, it was impossible to climb through this or any of the other gaps without snagging, soiling or otherwise damaging clothes.

An old man with a stick was being pushed and pulled through now, his face impassive as he endured this indignity and discomfort. Once he was finally down on the ground he hobbled off down the hill. A woman, from the country, judging by her intricately embroidered jilbeb, tried to climb through next. She appeared determined to climb through with her enormous sack of cabbage leaves balanced on her head. A youngish man in a suit, who had helped the old man through, was trying to persuade her to let him take the weight and swing the sack over. Standing securely on the little flat platform at the top of the gap, he was ideally situated to perform this small courtesy without difficulty, but it was clear she was not going to let him. Her dark weather-beaten face was a mask of blank stubbornness. However in the end she relented a little, grudgingly permitting him to guide her feet, and then accepting the hands that were reaching up to help her down safely.

Three women dressed head-to-toe in elegant hejebs and jil-bebs of high quality cloth were climbing through now. They must have been on their way to some important occasion, and may even have been important in themselves – they were being accorded a great deal of respect, and eagerly helped and assisted. The first woman was dressed in a lustrous blue jilbeb and matching scarf, and was red in the face from the effort required to haul herself up. She cut the palm of her hand, as Lev had done. Opening her bag, she took out a white handkerchief and dabbed at her wound ineffectually. The second woman, in cream and gold, was made of sterner stuff, shaking off offers of assistance. Successfully reaching the platform, she attempted a two-step descent, but her heels were too fragile and one broke as she hit the ground. She stumbled but managed to put her hand down hard on the ground to stop her herself falling completely. The third woman had reached the platform without Lev noticing her, so engrossed was he in watching what was happening to her friend. She had been watching too. She was very tall and younger than the other two. Supported by hands from below, and by her own rigidly locked elbows, she floated to earth, her lime green jilbeb fluttering gracefully behind her. The second woman was in trouble; she couldn't really walk. However the woman in blue had a pair of flat pumps in her handbag, which she offered to her. Lev watched them glide off down the broken road, consciously restoring their dignity as they went. The tall, younger woman in the lime green had a long grey mark across the bottom of her jilbeb.

Before joining the queue, Lev walked further up the steep hill beyond the mosque. The view one way was back towards Jerusalem and the golden glow of the Dome of the

Rock; the other way towards the Jordan Mountains beyond
the Dead Sea. At the centre of the second panorama was a
dark grey monolithic structure. Lev had heard of the new
security wall that was being built but had not realised it was
already a reality.

After a five-minute walk he reached it.

The slabs from which this barrier was made were simply
larger versions of those used to make the present one down
in Abou Dis. Easily nine metres high, each had, just beneath
its top edge, a little hole for the crane hook, instead of the
metal loop Lev had seen on the other barriers. The ground
beneath each plinth was completely flattened, levelled and
spread with sand so the slabs fitted flush, leaving no hint of
a gap to slip through. The hundred metre stretch of the wall
Lev was standing beside had been built in isolation; it stood
towering above him, solitary and menacing, ready to be
extended in both directions. The existing barrier across the
old shepherds' path would clearly be swept away by this
structure in the next few weeks.

Lev walked along the prepared ground where the wall
would soon be erected. Rubble, rubbish and the remains of
smashed and bulldozed buildings had been pushed to the
side, right and left. There had been no effort to clear up and
cart away. Huge piles had spilled down the slopes into the
surrounding fields of olive trees. Ancient stone walls had
been buried and crushed and healthy olive trees uprooted
and left to rot, the length of their roots testament to their
age. Some of these upturned trees would have been there
when the shepherds had brought their skins and cheese to
Jerusalem through Abou Dis.

The wall's future path had been cleared flat in readiness

for construction. Lev could see it rolling over the landscape
to the south. It looked like an unravelled roll of surgical
bandage.

\* \* \*

Returning to Abou Dis, Lev scrambled through the gap in
the barrier, taking care not to cut his hand again. On the
other side dozens of yellow minibuses were waiting.

'Ramallah?'

'You are going to Ramallah?'

'Yes.'

'You go with him.'

The Judean Desert hills had a faint down of green on
them after the rain of the last few days, softening their
harshness – miraculous, since they had seemed so entirely
devoid of any hint of vegetation just a couple of weeks
before, when Lev had driven through in Sami's cab.

Lev was surprised by how many Israeli settlements had
been established to the east, close to the Jordan Valley. Most
looked new, some were still under construction. There
appeared to be lot of current building activity. The difference between the settlements and the Arab towns was dra-
matic. Even in the middle of construction, the settlements
looked orderly and neat; toy-like almost. The settlements
were generally composed of rows of two-storey houses with
satellite dishes and solar panels on their red tiled roofs. The
pavements were intact and tidily swept, and the roads
smooth and unbroken. To Lev's puzzlement, they all
appeared to be deserted. In contrast, the Arab towns, busy
and full of people, were no more than unplanned groups of
flats of uneven heights, thin plaster barely concealing the

concrete beneath. Interspersed among the blocks was the odd shabby-looking two- or three-storey house, and the occasional bungalow in the old style, with deep ground-floor porches on all sides and roofs patched with corrugated iron. Unfinished buildings were common, rusting iron girders pointing out of flat roofs waiting for cash to be found to complete them. No pavement was unbroken – indeed, there were few pavements at all, and those roads that had been tarmacked were rutted and patched.

\* \* \*

Qalandia Checkpoint was at the centre of an area of land which had been cleared and flattened with careless ruthlessness, the ground torn up and scattered with puddles. This ravaged space was bordered by irregular heaps of rubble, in front of which was a high wire fence. On the day Lev passed through, black plastic bags, snared in the fence's mesh, snapped intermittently in the wind like pistol shots. The checkpoint was a maze of waist-high concrete blocks and barbed wire, with sodden plasterboards placed over puddles in an effort to keep feet dry and shoes clean. Finally there was a covered tarmac walkway, wide enough for single file only, where three child soldiers were checking IDs.

Here there were floodlights, a sandbagged sentry box and two netting clad watchtowers. One of the soldiers, a girl, was so small, and her rifle so big in comparison, that it was almost longer than she was tall; her adolescent arms were so thin that they looked as though they hadn't the strength to pick up her weapon and carry it, let alone put it to her shoulder and take aim. Another of the soldiers had shoulder-length hair tied in a bunch and poking at an angle out from under his helmet. He was standing behind a pile of sandbags, his M16 trained on the queue waiting to be checked. A white line had been painted on the rough ground, twenty or so paces from the sentry box, behind which the queue of people was forced to stand. The third soldier, who was clearly in charge, had tied on the side of his helmet a makeshift cockade of the same camouflage netting that draped the watchtowers and sentry boxes. He sported it as if it were a favour thrown to him by some fine lady from a medieval balcony, prior to him leaving for battle. He used the open and shut fist gesture which Lev was now so familiar with to call each person towards him.

Alongside the walkway was a road where another group of soldiers was checking and searching each vehicle. The queues in both directions were long, and moving so slowly that some drivers were standing around or sitting on the bonnets of their cars, smoking and chatting.

When summoned, Lev handed over his passport as requested. The soldier looked at it with exaggerated interest.

'You are from?'

'England.'

'Ah, the UK. You are from?'

'England!'

'No, today?'

'Oh I see. Jerusalem.'

'You live there?'

'No I live in London. At the moment I am staying with my sister in Rehavia.'

'Ah! Rehavia. You are going to?'

'Ramallah.'

'Why?'

'To see.'

'Tourist?'

'Visitor.'

'You are a Jew?'

'I am.'

'It is dangerous for us in Ramallah these days.'

'I'll be alright, don't worry.'

'Why don't you go to Tel Aviv?'

'I've been there. I've not been to Ramallah.'

'You know someone in Ramallah?'

'No.'

'No one?'

'No.'

'Why do you go there then?'

'To see only.'

'I see.'

He looked back at the boy with the M16, whose face remained impassive.

'OK. Have a nice day.'

'Thanks.'

Lev took his passport back.

'There was trouble there last night.'

'I know.'

'Be careful.'

'I will.'

∗ ∗ ∗

'Ramallah. Ramallah. Sirda. Sirda.'

Lev didn't know where Sirda was so he jumped in the last available seat of a minibus going to Ramallah. Full, it drew away almost immediately.

He asked the man sitting beside him how much the fare was.

'Two shekels.'

The man had his own fare ready in his hand. He took Lev's and passed them both through to the driver. He looked deeply at Lev and, very seriously, said, 'Together. The best way.'

He then patted Lev companionably on his knee. He said nothing more for the rest of the ten minute journey. It had taken twenty minutes from Abou Dis to Qalandia; Lev had been at the checkpoint for more than forty minutes.

Ramallah was in mourning.

When the minibus stopped and he got out with the rest of the passengers, Lev knew immediately. The streets were full of people in little groups, smoking and talking quietly. The shops were all closed, the shutters pasted with posters carrying images of the dead. Lev had lied at the checkpoint; he had often been to Ramallah – although not for twenty-five years. As a student, he and his friends and Udi used to motor up there from Jerusalem for a night out. In those days it was full of clubs and restaurants. Lev remembered a busy, happy town crowded with people and hooting cars.

This morning Ramallah was hushed with sadness.

The posters were visible not only on the shutters of every shop but on the windscreens of cars, the sides of vans, plastered on walls. Simple in design, they had been produced in just a few hours – the five had died late the night before, and it was now only just a little after ten in the morning. One or two were beginning to peel away, the gum no doubt cheap and hurriedly applied. The faces of the slaughtered mugshotted out at Lev everywhere he went, their accusatory gazes the result of the photobooth's flash rather than the defiance which, at first sight, their eyes seemed to suggest. Five separate posters had been produced: in each, the image of the dead was surrounded by a quotation from the Koran, an exhortation not to give into the oppression, a short eulogy about the particular individual, and the place, date and time of the death and how it had happened. Each carried a vehement condemnation of Israel and all Israelis.

It was clear that any activity in Ramallah that day was taking place far from the cluttered little roundabouts which were its usual busy nuclei. Lev drifted with the crowds. Hundreds of people had gathered around a mosque close to the deserted vegetable-market. The crowd was mixed: men, women and children, young and old. An ambulance and two vans were parked outside. The mosque was packed; those unable to get in had to stand outside on the street. Each of the vehicles was plastered with posters. Around them, propped up against walls, were banners and the flags of the Palestinian Authority and Hamas.

A group of children were pointing at a poster of the nine-year-old who had died. No more than nine themselves, they were here because the schools too had been closed for the day. Lev watched them, unable to read in their faces their reactions to what they were looking at. Death must have been so much part of their lives, they heard about it all the time. They nudged each other, pushed and pinched, and, giggling, disappeared into the crowd.

Then, as if in sympathy, the weather closed in. It had been bright enough when Lev had gone through Qalandia, but dark, mournful clouds now filled the sky, so low that the crescents on the mosque's minarets were obscured. Rain started, first a drizzle and then a downpour, and in minutes the streets were streaming with water. In a hopeless attempt to protect themselves, some put shoeboxes on their heads, others paper hats, handbags, plastic shopping bags. All were useless, so dense was the downpour. Taking cover under what little shelter was available, Lev stepped into a torrent from a pipe that must have broken the moment he stepped back. Everyone around him laughed good-humouredly. Their capacity for sturdy resiliance amazed him. He laughed too.

From the mosque came the bodies, wrapped in cloths the same green as the Hamas and Arab League flags, and bound tight to stretchers. The nine-year-old was no more than a wretched little bundle. There was crying, screams of anguish and low moaning. Megaphones appeared. The slogans began. Young men in black balaclavas with rifles over their shoulders led the procession. Fusillades of shots were fired into the air. The three vehicles were there to serve as hearses, but for much of the way to the cemetery the bodies were borne on the shoulders of mourners. Banners were lifted high and flags were waved to the rhythm of the messages being repeated through the megaphones: 'They have not died in vain'; 'The Jews will be banished from Palestinian land, the battle will continue until they are'; 'The dead are even now in their resting place in heaven'; 'In sacrifice they are our heroes'; 'God is one and indivisible.'

The procession reached the main street; there, the numbers were at their greatest, the megaphone exhortations at their loudest, the stamping rhythm of revenge most insistent. But as the cemetery neared, the vengeful refrains became sporadic and the crowd slowly diminished, leaving family and friends to their private grief. The banners, megaphones and weapons disappeared; balaclavas were pocketed, and the young militants faded quietly away.

Lev walked back to the centre of Ramallah. The route of the procession was littered with discarded flag batons. The rain was still heavy, and the ground was filthy. Lev felt lonely and exposed. There was nowhere open to eat, or even buy a tea. He asked the whereabouts of the house that had been attacked the night before. His Arabic was returning; he was beginning to be understood immediately now.

'Take a cab. Ask for Maroun.'

He couldn't remember much grammar but he was surprised how much vocabulary he could dredge up. There were very few cabs around, but after ten minutes one drifted along the street towards him. The driver looked at him suspiciously when he asked to be taken to Maroun. He had been identified for what he was, but the driver indicated that he should get in nevertheless. Lev was anxious lest he should be challenged, and at a loss as to what to say if he was. The journey through the deserted streets to Maroun only took a few minutes.

In places, Ramallah was very gracious, with wide, tree-lined avenues and prosperous-looking houses surrounded by high-walled compounds. Otherwise it resembled the Arab towns he had passed earlier that day. As they slowed, for the third or fourth time, to negotiate a particularly rough piece of broken tarmac, Lev ventured to ask his driver why the roads were so torn and potholed.

'Israeli tanks.'

'When?'

'Most nights.'

'Most nights?'

'Yes. You never leave us in peace. Why don't you leave us in peace?'

His Jewishness openly acknowledged for the first time that day, Lev turned to look at the driver.

'I can only say how sorry I am. I can offer you no excuses.'

'You don't live here?'

'No, in London.'

'Ah.'

Maroun was a wealthy suburb of Ramallah – new blocks of flats, villas with large well-tended gardens. The building that had been attacked turned out to be an eight-storey block of spacious apartments. The building was now a wreck, almost completely demolished; not even a shell remained. Only one outside wall still stood, to the height of what had been the fourth floor. The ruin was steaming after the rain, and was still being picked over when Lev arrived. Firemen were digging up and sorting through the debris and shining torches into cavities. There was still a possibility that there were bodies to be found. Schoolbooks, ragged prayer mats, cushions, shoes, battered kitchen bowls and the yellow foam from busted mattresses littered the razed site. The handles of a holdall were uncovered and it was eagerly extricated from the rubble in the hope that there was something salvageable inside, but it was empty and thrown down in disappointment.

Lev was shocked beyond words at the devastation. The attack must have been totally indiscriminate, and the munitions hugely powerful to cause such comprehensive damage. Glass in the windows of adjoining buildings had been shattered by the blasts, and the tiles on the roof of an old house two streets down the hill had been blown away.

The scene was bleak and hopeless, like nothing Lev had seen before. As he scrambled over the piles of smashed masonry, picking his way through the sodden remains of what, only yesterday, had been half a dozen cosy homes, the sun was setting under the dark rain clouds and the horizon was brilliantly lit. For just a few moments it was as if an angry fire was burning behind the gentle hills of central Palestine. The slim strip of burning light resembled the entrance to an inferno.

A faint, warm drizzle had begun. Lev fled from the site, chilled to his marrow. He began to shiver. Nablus would have to wait.

The taxi was still there. Like Lev, the driver had been wandering sadly around, shaking his head from time to time, talking to the firefighters, sharing his cigarettes. Lev stumbled across to him, mumbling and stammering, barely managing to make himself understood.

'A hotel please. Could you take me to a hotel? I need to leave. I have to go.'

The driver nodded.

'You are alright?'

'Yes I'm fine. I'm fine.'

Lev turned away and looked back at the devastation behind him.

'I'm so sorry. I'm so sorry for all of this.'

'Now you see how we live.'

Immediately after booking in, Lev went straight to bed. He found himself shivering still, and he continued to shake until falling into a fitful sleep which lasted until morning.

* * *

The dawn sky was blue. From nine the sun was warm, and the shops in central Ramallah were open again from ten. The town was all buzz and noise. Lev got himself a shave and then a bagel and a coffee, and walked to the place where the minibus had dropped him the day before. The shave was not a great success. The young guy who had done it had nicked him a couple of times and had found some difficulty sealing the cuts and staunching the bleeding.

'Nablus?'

'Nablus?'

'Yes Nablus. Is that possible?'

'Yes.'

'Where do I go from?'

'Sirda. You need to go to Sirda.'

'Not direct to Nablus?'

'No, Sirda.'

'OK, Sirda then.'

'Not here.'

'Then where?'

'Sirda bus over there.'

Lev walked to the other side of the roundabout.

'Sirda?'

'You want to go to Sirda?'

'No Nablus.'

'You must go to Sirda first and then to Nablus.'

'Fine. Sirda bus here?'

'Yes. Here Sirda bus.'

He got on, sitting down on the last vacant seat, the fold-down one beside the door.

Sirda Checkpoint was only a few kilometres outside Ramallah. That morning it was unusually crowded. Those who had to travel were taking advantage of the absence of the Israeli soldiers who normally monitored this stretch of road, the only route Palestinians were permitted to take going north out of the town. The checkpoint was very different from Qalandia. At both ends of a sweeping stretch of road with olive trees on either side were two rough piles of concrete. The minibus had dropped Lev some way before the first and he had to thread his way to it through other minibuses, and stalls selling food, drinks, cigarettes and gaily-coloured cushions. Neither barrier was high and passageways had been cleared, wide enough to walk through easily, even with bags and bundles. Such was the number of people going both ways that there was still congestion and queues, even without the usual Israeli checks. The distance between the two piles of concrete was at least a kilometre, and someone had brought four ponies and a couple of traps and was ferrying travellers between them. There was a fair-like atmosphere, and in the way that those at fairs are determined to have a good time, the people here seemed determined not to let all this inconvenience get them down. Everyone was conscientiously good-humoured at Sirda.

On the other side of the second pile of concrete were more minibuses.

'Nablus?' Lev asked.

'No Nablus, Za'tara. Za'tara first.'

'OK. Bus to Za'tara here?'

'There.'

'Where?'

'There.'

Lev walked up the hill out of the valley and asked again.

'Za'tara?'

'Here Za'tara.'

It appeared not many people were going to Za'tara, and he had to wait for half an hour until his minibus was full.

Leaving the Sirda valley behind, the bus drove through a succession of similar valleys, all planted with olive trees. They passed the odd desolate Arab town, where people seemed to be doing no more than scratching a living. On the top of most of the hills were Israeli settlements, looking like so many yarmulkes, neat but precarious and just about to topple off. Tidy affronts to the natural wildness of the area, the bright red roofs jarred against the rocky landscape and grey-green olive trees that surrounded them. The Arab towns, as scruffy and plain ugly as most of them were, looked rooted, as if they had been there always, and would be there for ever.

Entering a bigger-than-average village, the minibus turned sharp left, uphill. The driver had been explaining to his passengers that he couldn't take the normal route because Israeli soldiers had recently blocked it. However, a young boy jumped out from a shop doorway and waved them down. There was a conversation between him and the driver, resulting in the minibus backing up to the junction and driving off in another direction. The locals had apparently cleared the new roadblock away, and the normal route was now clear. It proved to be much smoother, the tarmac less broken – a main road, if not a highway – and they began to make fast progress.

The roadblock turned out to be still substantially in place but it was no more than a succession of hastily piled heaps of debris strewn across the carriageway; the width of a single vehicle had been cleared to one side. Lev's fellow passengers, and especially the driver, seemed to tense as soon as they passed through. Since the road had been blocked, they were probably not permitted to drive along this particular stretch.

They had not travelled more than fifty metres beyond the barrier when another minibus, just like theirs, drove round a corner straight at them, flashing its lights. Their driver immediately understood the significance and shuddered to an abrupt halt. He reversed back a few metres and drove off the road down a rough track among the olives. The other minibus followed. The two drivers were both driving very fast and recklessly. When the track took a sharp turn into a shallow trench between two small slopes of olive trees, both vehicles slammed to an abrupt halt. A passenger from the other minibus leapt out and ran up the slope nearest to the main road. He came back almost immediately and both vehicles took off again, slower this time. Everyone was looking towards the main road, craning, peering, trying to look through the tangle of olive tree branches. No one seemed frightened exactly, just alert, edgy. No one spoke. The driver pointed. Everyone strained to see what he had spotted. Cruising slowly along the main road was an Israeli armoured vehicle. It was hide and seek and they had not been discovered. The Israeli soldiers drove on and disappeared. As the distance between them and the army truck grew, the tension among the passengers was slowly released and there was clapping and laughing at the hollow little victory.

Despite the disappearance of the Israelis the driver didn't return to the main road immediately but drove along a track, which wound its way through two more little valleys.

In the second was a Bedouin camp, their goats and sheep grazing under the olive trees. These were the first Bedouin Lev had seen since arriving; he seemed to remember seeing many more such camps as a child. There was so much Lev wanted to ask, but he had no idea what the reaction of his fellow passengers would be were they to discover that he was Jewish.

The driver seemed to know his way because he took a succession of sidetracks and eventually came back up onto the main road. A road sign showed that Za'tara was now only a few kilometres further on. They could not allow themselves to be seen by the soldiers at the Za'tara Checkpoint to be approaching along the main road. The driver took a turning through another cleared mound of debris and came down to the roadblock from the hillside so that it appeared they were coming from a little Arab village that was situated nearby. The minibus stopped some way off; the driver didn't want to risk being questioned by the soldiers. The passengers all got out without complaint and trooped wearily towards the maze of concrete blocks, barriers, barbed wire and watchtowers. Small queues of vehicles and long lines of people were waiting to be checked on either side.

\* \* \*

Za'tara Checkpoint was on a major intersection, with roads going four ways: to Tel Aviv, Ramallah, Nablus and down to the Jordan Valley. It was in a wide, generous dish of land in the middle of the hills. Watching over it all was a large artillery piece, dug into an artificial mound.

There was a red line in the asphalt. One by one each person in the queue was beckoned from behind it. Lev looked at his watch; it was almost exactly midday. The sun was bright rather than hot. There were no girl soldiers here; all were boys, and they appeared to want to play the fool rather than seriously check anyone, talking and joking among themselves, showing off. They barely looked at Lev's passport. Nevertheless it was a very slow process. They were having such a good time that they occasionally forgot to beckon anyone forward at all. Those forced to wait stood patiently in line, watching the soldiers' antics stoically.

Once he was through, Lev got in a minibus to Hawara, which was supposed to be near to the next checkpoint. Lev had to wait as his minibus filled up, but he was grateful for the chance to review his day so far and catch his breath. He sat watching the queue of people straggling through, tired and dirty. Soon the minibus was full. On his Israeli map Hawara wasn't even marked. Apparently it was only a few kilometres outside Nablus. Lev was never to find out precisely how many.

* * *

The checkpoint near Hawara looked much the same as the checkpoint at Qalandia, except that the queues were immense, both for pedestrians and for vehicles. As at Sirda, stalls had been set up, selling hot and cold food and drinks. There were many more armoured vehicles and tanks than at Qalandia and there were no disconsolate soldiers wandering about smoking. None were fooling around; instead they were alert and watchful. For the first time since he left Ramallah, Lev felt intimidated. An atmosphere of threat and repression hung over this checkpoint.

After waiting for over an hour Lev found himself approaching another line on the ground; this one was white, and behind it was a wide, cleared space. What he watched taking place on this stage was clearly routine; the actors knew their roles.

One man though, two or three people in front of Lev in the line, didn't wait long enough for his cue, crossing the white line before he was beckoned. He was halted abruptly with a screamed shout and sent to one side to wait, punished, it appeared, for his audacity. He slouched across to a low brick wall, swung his legs over and sat with his back to the soldiers. Slumping his elbows on to his knees he looked out across the low Palestinian hills to the east, his head cocked defiantly, his neck deep in his shoulders betraying his surrender. He joined three others. A tented shelter had been rigged up to protect them from the sun. None of them had chosen to make use of it.

A young woman with two children, carrying several packages and bags, was instructed to deposit her luggage between the white line and the soldiers, and then told to back away behind the white line again. She was questioned about her luggage's contents, in a yelled mixture of Hebrew, Arabic and English. The young soldiers weren't satisfied with what she told them so they shouted instructions to her to come forward again and open her parcels and bags. Still dissatisfied, they yelled at her to empty one of her shoulder bags onto the filthy ground.

Lev watched young men being told to pirouette with their coats and sweaters lifted above their waist, exposing their bare midriffs to show they carried no weapons. To hide their self-consciousness, some twisted balletically. Lev watched as older men with paunches were told to unbuckle their belts and open the front of their trousers to prove that it was just their stomach that bulked out their clothing and not something more sinister. If they hesitated, as most did, they were chivvied raucously. One of the young soldiers shouted out in English, 'hurry up old man, get a move on.' The man in question, tall and distinguished-looking, was making a mess of unzipping his flies; his shoulders were shaking with shame and confusion.

Lev was recognised even at twenty metres as different from the rest. He was called forward. He proffered his passport. The young soldier spoke in Hebrew after looking at it only briefly.

'You are a Jew.'

It was a statement rather than an enquiry.

'Yes.'

'You are from?'

'England, but today from Jerusalem.'

'You go to?'

'Nablus.'

'Why?'

'To visit the Old Town. I want to stay for a couple of days. Go up to Mount Gerizim, perhaps go to Sebastiya.'

'Why?'

'These are very important, famous sites. I am interested in archaeology.'

'What are they, these places?'

'You don't know? Well Sebastiya is the old capital of ancient Samaria and Mount ...'

The soldier wasn't listening, he was looking down at Lev's passport again, scrutinising the stamped entry visa.

He was short and fat, and so fair that his eyebrows were almost invisible against his skin. He looked back up. His eyes were a very pale, colourless blue.

'Lev.'

'Yes?'

'Why do you really want to go to Nablus?'

'I told you …'

'Why does any Jew want to go to Nablus?'

'What are you getting at?'

'Except to make trouble.'

'I don't follow. As I told you before, there are some very interesting places to visit there. There's a place called Jacob's Well, too. It's a Greek Orthodox—'

The young soldier waved his hand in front of Lev's face dismissively.

'Nablus is very dangerous. There are many terrorists there. You'll not be safe. You will be in danger.'

'I'll be careful. I'll be alright.'

'How? You have somewhere to stay? Do you know someone in Nablus?'

'No.'

'Any Palestinians?'

'No.'

'Do you work for any Palestinian organisation?'

'No. I'm a Jew.'

'Some Jews do.'

'What?'

'Work for Palestinian organisations.'

'Do they?'

'Yes. Didn't you know?'

'No. I live in England now.'

'In London?'

'Yes.'

'It is a famous place.'

'Yes. Yes it is.'

'These places you want to visit, they are famous?'

'Very.'

'I've not heard of them.'

'I'm surprised if you haven't.'

'I haven't.'

Standing further back was another young soldier, tall and languid, with curly hair in braids and a beret rather than a helmet. He seemed to be finding the interrogation amusing. He coughed and the soldier who had been questioning Lev turned round and glanced at him. The soldier in the beret gestured with a turn of an outstretched hand and a pursing of his lips, as if to say "Why not? Let him through." The pale young soldier turned back to Lev.

'You are a tourist?'

'Yes, you could call me that.'

'And you are a Jew.'

'I am.'

'A Jewish tourist from London.'

'That's right.'

'A Jew who wants to visit Nablus.'

'Yes.'

'I see.'

'Is there a problem?'

Lev could sense his uncertainty. Again he glanced back, and again his colleague pursed his lips, more non-committally than before. The young soldier, until then so unsure, suddenly made up his mind.

'Yes there is. I'm not going to let you through. You must go back.'

'I beg your pardon?'

'Go back. I'm telling you to go back.'

'But I've come a long way I've been through three check-points to get this far, and there's been no problem. Why here?'

'This is Hawara.'

'What's so different about Hawara?'

His languid colleague chipped in.

'No tourists or terrorists allowed through Hawara.'

He grinned broadly.

'Can I see your commanding officer?'

'I'm in charge here. Go back. I'm telling you to go back. Shalom. Have a nice day.'

There was quiet support from behind.

'Don't make it difficult for us Lev. We have our orders.'

Lev addressed him directly. 'You'd have let me through though wouldn't you? If it weren't for him you would have let me through. I know you would. I've come a long way today.'

The soldier with the near-invisible eyebrows stepped sharply to one side, almost coming to attention, as if he was suddenly on the parade ground.

'It's not up to him. I'm in charge here. Go back. Go back now. Do you hear? I'm ordering you to go back.'

He pulled his rifle off his shoulder.

The voice intoned softly from behind. 'Go back Lev. It's easier that way.'

'Now. Do you hear? Now. I will not let you through and that's final.'

Lev turned away. 'But—'

'Thanks Lev.' It was the soft voice again.

Lev had been alone for the best part of two days, but he had never felt quite so alone as he did walking back past the long queue of people and the makeshift stalls at the checkpoint near Hawara. He felt diminished, almost as if he was guilty of some offence and was being punished. He was being looked at, but with curiosity rather than ridicule. Some showed concern; one or two asked him what had happened; a couple of men touched him consolingly on his shoulder.

When he finally reached the end of the queue and came level with the line of minibuses, he was approached by a man in a torn white shirt and green chinos. Tall and very strong, with a well-defined body, he spoke to Lev softly.

'The soldiers, have the soldiers turned you back?'

'Yes.'

'Don't worry, it happens to us all the time.'

Lev looked up at him. His eyes were frank and warm. His shaven head shone in the afternoon sun.

'I'm not used to it.'

The big man smiled down at Lev.

'Stay in Palestine long enough and it'll be a daily experience. Do you still want to go to Nablus? There's another checkpoint at Awerta. You can try there.'

Lev wasn't sure.

'Fifteen shekels and I bring you back here if you don't get through. If the soldiers turn you back there as well I bring you back here. No extra charge. Fifteen shekels all in, one-way or return, it doesn't matter.' He laughed. 'You understand me?'

Lev still wasn't sure. 'One-way or return and no extra charge?'

'That's it.' The large man smiled encouragingly. 'What you got to lose?'

'You're quite right there. Alright it's a deal. Why not?'

'Come this way. Come with me.'

Lev followed him obediently to a ramshackle vehicle, the seats all torn, the bodywork rusty. He assumed it was a taxi, although it was not marked as one. It rattled noisily as they passed through a grubby little collection of drab buildings, which it seemed was Hawara Town. They turned left down a rough track between old stone walls and drove for ten minutes before topping a ridge and descending into a dusty valley. The hills were more like mountains, less gentle than earlier in the day. It was now well after two in the afternoon.

* * *

Awerta Checkpoint was small and isolated, the road through it no more than a wide, rough track. There was a small queue of trucks and vans waiting to go through to Nablus. None were waiting to come out.

'I wait for you here. See what happens.'

They had stopped a hundred metres away from the checkpoint. Lev thanked him and handed over the fare. He made his way towards the soldiers. Unlike Hawara there were no queues of pedestrians. Only one man on foot was waiting to go through. He was opening his packages under the distant eyes of two soldiers and a watchtower with a slim gun turret. The soldiers appeared to be asking the man to open his clothing as they had at Hawara. He was arguing that he was only wearing a shirt under his jacket. He took it off to show them that it was impossible for him to be hiding anything. Satisfied, they beckoned him forward, checked his ID and let him go through.

Lev began walking towards them. He was stopped with a flat palm.

'You are?'

'I'm English. I'm going to Nablus.'

They called him to come closer and one of them took his passport. Hardly looking at anything other than the front cover, he glanced up at Lev warily.

'No tourists allowed in Nablus.'

'I've come a long way.'

'You're a Jew, right?'

'Yes.'

'You speak Hebrew?'

'Yes, and English.'

The youthful, spotty face brightened a little.

'That's OK then. My Arabic's hopeless and my Hebrew's not much better. Look, you can't go into Nablus. We've orders not to let any internationals through unless they've got a permit or they are pilgrims.'

'I want to see Jacob's Well. Does that make me pilgrim?'

'You do? Really?'

'Yes.'

'You have a letter? Pilgrims usually come in groups and have letters.'

'No. I've no letter I'm afraid.'

'You should have a letter, from your bishop.'

'I'm a Jew.'

'From the rabbi?'

The young soldier looked doubtful about this as soon as he had said it.

'I haven't got anything. I'm sorry, I didn't know I had to have a letter.'

'Look I'll check for you. Jacob's Well you say.'

'Yes.'

'What is it?'

'You don't know? It's a Greek Orthodox Church. It's supposed to stand over the site of—'

'Why does a Jew want to go to Greek Orthodox Church?'

'It's famous.'

'It is? I've not heard of it. It doesn't matter. Stand over there.'

'Where?'

'Over there.'

He pointed to a patch of flat ground to one side of the pathway, near some rocks. Lev went and stood where he was told.

'Not there. Further back.'

Lev backed off.

'That's OK. I'll go and check now.'

Lev thanked him but they were probably too far apart now for him to have heard. The soldier disappeared into a tent. An adjustable pole with a mirror leant against it. The other soldier stood watching him, smoking. It seemed there were only the two of them, although there could have been others in the cabin on top of the watchtower. Both soldiers were thin and boyish: adolescent arms, hollow chests, slim waists. Their uniforms hung off their gawky young bodies, and their boots seemed too big for their scrawny legs. While

Lev was being dealt with, the queue of vehicles had grown longer and there was now one truck waiting on the other side, coming out of Nablus.

The young soldier emerged from the tent. He shouted across.

'They are going to call me back. Please wait. OK?'

'OK.'

The two soldiers then went together over to the truck that was leaving Nablus and asked for the driver's papers. Lev looked back down the track. His driver was patiently waiting, leaning against his car. After a few minutes there was a high-pitched ringing from the tent.

The soldier left the truck and went back into his tent. He came out again almost immediately. He yelled.

'I'm sorry you must go back. That was my instructions. No internationals in Nablus today.'

He turned away and went back to join the other soldier, picking up the pole with the mirror as he went. Lev had been dismissed.

'No good?' said the taxi driver.

'No good.'

'Not so bad this time?'

'No, not so bad.'

Lev threw his bag on the back seat and lit a cigarette. He was tired now, tired and dejected.

'Now you see how we live.'

'What?'

'We must live like this. I can't go to Nablus either. I have no permit. I go but I must go through the hills, the back way. If I'm caught, if the soldiers catch me …'

He did a slip slapping motion in the air.

'You understand me?'

'Perfectly.'

They drove off back down the road.

'You still want to go to Nablus today?'

'Yes I do. I certainly don't want to go back to Ramallah. That would completely depress me. I think I'd scream. Yes I want to beat this. If there's a way?'

'There's a way, believe me. I take you.'

'Through the hills?'

'That's it. Through the hills.'

'Is it safe?'

'Everyone does it. The Israelis don't want anyone to go to Nablus.'

'Why?'

'They think it's a base for terrorists.'

They had in the meantime driven back through Hawara and arrived back at the checkpoint. Lev had thought that they would be going together through the hills to Nablus; he was wrong. When they stopped, his new friend pointed at the line of minibuses.

'That bus there. The one almost full of people. It'll take you. Five shekels only.'

'Are you sure?'

'I'm sure. Don't worry.'

'Is it dangerous?'

'Palestine is dangerous.'

Lev was beyond caring. He turned in his seat.

'Thank you for all your help. You have been very kind.' He splayed his hand in the centre of his chest and gently inclined his head. 'My name is Lev.'

His big companion returned the gesture with a delicacy
and grace that belied his size.

'I am Omar'

'Thanks, Omar.'

Before Lev got out of the car they shook hands.

'Be careful, Lev. When you're in the minibus, do what
everyone else does and question nothing. There will not be
time.'

*  *  *

Approaching the minibus Lev spoke quietly to the driver.

'Nablus?'

'Nablus. Get in.'

After collecting fares, the driver set off, turning right just
before reaching Hawara. He was racing. Everyone inside was
craning forward, watchful and alert. Suddenly the bus U-
turned and shuddered to an abrupt stop, the door was slid
back and everyone leapt out and ran across the road and
began running up a steep slope. After a second's hesitation
Lev followed. Behind them the minibus, with a screech of its
tyres, sped away back towards Hawara; the driver didn't even
wait around long enough to slide the passenger door closed.
The bank had turned into hillside, the top of which seemed
to Lev a very long way off. He was quickly becoming out of
breath. He began wheezing. He hadn't been prepared for
this. Everything was happening too quickly.

Looking across at those who were running with him, Lev
realised they were all much younger than him. Nevertheless,
they were all by now red in the face and rapidly faltering,
their pace slackening. Despite their tiredness, some were

looking anxiously back at the road, while others were scanning the sky. Eventually, one by one, they reached the top, so exhausted by now that they fell and rolled rather than ran down the other side. At the bottom they piled into a battered white van without seats or windows. The driver looked on edge, and as soon as the first of them appeared he had started the engine. As the last of them got in, he drove off straightaway. Someone slid the door closed. Suddenly it was pitch black. There was laughter. Another little victory?

The driver drove furiously; the van's axle continually struck the ground as the van careered uphill. The driver appeared not to notice. Inside they were jolted and shaken around. Lev parted a little curtain that separated the passengers from the driver and tried to look through the windscreen. They were driving up a track which from time to time was little more than a footpath. After four or five minutes they reached a tarmacked road and the driver drew back the curtain. A dim light illuminated the back of the van. Smiling over his shoulder at them with relief, he slowed down and began to drive more carefully.

Lev found that he was sitting next to a young man, who was looking at him intently.

Lev smiled at him. 'I don't understand what's happening.'

'You a Jew?'

'No, English. From London.'

Lev felt a flush of shame suffuse his face. He was relieved that they were still in semi-darkness; it was unlikely that any of the other passengers had noticed his discomfort. His firm denial seemed effective; he was now just a foreigner who happened to look Jewish.

'You are welcome.'

'Thank you.'

'You speak Arabic?'

'A few words only.'

'I am a student of English. My name is Walid. We can speak English.'

'Thank you. My name is Lev.'

Lev swallowed his name as he said it. Walid didn't appear to pick up on his careless slip.

Walid was a very serious, nervous young man, with bright inquisitive eyes and a feeble little beard.

'So what's happening Walid?'

'The first road after Hawara Village was an Israeli road.'

'An Israeli road?'

'We are not allowed there; the minibus was not allowed there, Israeli vehicles only. That's why the driver turned round before he let us out, so that he could get away quickly, before he was seen. If he had gone another kilometre the soldiers at the settlement might have caught sight of him. And then, well, anything can happen. Our driver is from a village near here, he is not from Nablus. He's not taking us there. He'll take us only some of the way. He spends his day waiting for groups like us. Sometimes there are helicopters and they see him. Then it can be difficult. He has to find an excuse for waiting there. He has sheep.'

Walid spread his hands, palms up, as if sheep could be an excuse for anything.

'You were turned back at Hawara?' he said.

'Yes.'

'None of us even try to get through there.'

'Why?'

'None of us has a permit to enter Nablus. So we have to get in this way.'

'How often do you go through this?'

'Some of us do it everyday.'

'Why do you bother if it's so difficult?'

'We work in Nablus, we've got jobs there.'

'Yet you still can't get a permit?'

'No.'

'Why?'

'The Israelis say it's for security reasons.'

'So you've all applied?'

'Most of us have.'

'And been turned down?'

'Yes.'

'So that means by still going to Nablus you are putting yourself in danger, you are breaking the law.'

Walid laughed. He translated what Lev had said to everyone else in the van. They all laughed too.

'Whose law? Not ours.'

Lev flushed red for a second time, he felt suddenly very stupid.

'I must seem so naive to you all.'

'You are from overseas. No one there really understands how we live here. Some of us feel none of you much care either.'

'Some of us do.'

'I'm glad.'

'Are we safe now?'

'Now we are OK. This is a farm road; the driver is allowed to be here.'

'What he does is very dangerous?'

'That is why we must each pay him fifteen shekels.'

'He could get shot at?'

'Yes. His brother was killed six months ago.'

'Doing this?'

'Yes. Of course.'

'There are only ten of us in here. He risks getting killed for 150 shekels?'

'What can he do?'

'That's little more than nine or ten English pounds!'

'He can do ten trips a day both ways.'

'Risking death for only £200 a day!'

The van was slowing.

'We must get out and walk now.'

'Why?'

'No road. Israeli tanks. Last night a couple of them broke up the road.'

'Why?'

Walid heaved his shoulders up to his ears and sighed expressively.

'To make our lives even more difficult? We now have to walk to the next village rather than ride.'

'Is it far?'

'Not far. There, you can see it. Look. It is not too far. Two or three kilometres?'

The sun had gone now and it was cold. In the gathering gloom it was difficult to pick a way through the rubble. Both the tarmac and the original foundation brick had been torn up. Another minibus, yellow like all legitimate minibuses, was waiting for them on the outskirts of the next settlement. They were driven quickly down the hill into central Nablus.

It was now seven p.m. The distance from Ramallah to

Nablus on the main highway was fifty kilometres, according to Lev's map. It used to take just over an hour when Lev had gone there as a teenager. Today it had taken him nine hours.

He got out and stood in the centre of a bustling crowd.

Everything that had happened to him since he had left Rehavia two days before bewildered him. He was surprised that, though at times he had been in real danger, he had seldom felt frightened. He could have been arrested, even ended up in jail. Worse, he could have been injured, and today he could even have died. Yet still he had felt no real fear. Was it because so much of what he had experienced had been so unexpected, and had happened so fast? Or just that there had been no time to think about being scared? Or was it simply that the nature of the threat was so random – whimsical almost, when the soldiers felt safe; so implacably oppressive when they didn't – that fear offered no protection?

He was exhausted now, but elated. He had won hadn't he? His own little victory. He was in Nablus. Yet he had denied his Jewishness in the process, something he had not done before.

And now? Now he had to eat and find somewhere to sleep. Walid was late for something, he said, but before leaving he took the trouble to give Lev precise directions to a nearby hotel.

*  *  *

The next morning was bright and very warm. Lev had slept soundly in the place Walid had recommended, and had eaten well. He had shared a table with another guest, a woman, who said she was sixty-five but who looked considerable older. Her name was Margarette. She told Lev she was a freelancer for a Swiss news agency. Her neat grey hair, worn tidily swept up and clipped at the back of her bird-like head, gave lie to the fierce passion she soon displayed.

'I've been amazed at how patient and forbearing the ordinary, everyday Palestinian is,' said Lev, 'how orderly. For those old Arab men, patriarchs in their own families, respected and looked up to, it must be very difficult to be ordered about, made to wait in queues and constantly checked by these child soldiers young enough to be their grandchildren. Yet they appeared to put up with it.'

'In my articles over the years I have sometimes described these old men as possessing 'tolerant impassivity'. Imagine, too, how it can be for the teenagers, for the young men and women who have toe the line to please Israeli soldiers barely older than themselves?'

'It must be a very bitter experience. Yet they have to get on with their lives, don't they? Go to college, get to their jobs punctually, all the normal things.'

'And that means daily acceptance, resignation, expedient conformity. If they are too overtly truculent they will be delayed or even turned back altogether.'

'I went to a funeral in Ramallah you know.'

'Did you indeed?'

'Hamas was there, shouting through megaphones.'

'Of course.'

'I understand now why those Hamas megaphone exhortations were so urgent, so raucous and extreme in their sentiments. The temptation for ordinary people, like the ones I saw coming through at Za'tara, tired and dusty and just wanting to go home, to take the line of least resistance must be a very strong habit and very difficult to break. On one hand these people's resilience is admirable, but on the other, to the activists, it must be shocking. To an activist it's imperative, isn't it, that they are jerked out of their passivity?'

'That's how Hamas sees it, certainly.'

'That was why, for an activist, the funeral in Ramallah had to be hijacked for a short time at least.'

'It was an opportunity to remind people of the repression they are living under and that they should not accept it as their fate.'

'But are they right, the activists? Are they right to want to turn admirable resilience into constant resistance?'

'Do they have an alternative?'

'"Takes two", Jack said.'

'Jack?'

'A friend. I'm on my way to see his brother. That's where I'm going ... What I mean is that the Israeli authorities should be responding to how these people, the sort of people I've seen today, are behaving rather than to how the activists behave. By failing to respond to them, aren't we pushing them into the arms of the activists?'

'I have been writing about Palestine for twenty years. On and off for twenty years. More. And what real effect have I had? The difficulty for me has always been about getting the balance right: cite every awful detail and the "breakfast cereal readers", as I call them, say to themselves, "This just can't be true"; temper my descriptions and they say to themselves, "It's not as bad all that then, is it?" I don't know whether I have ever managed to get it right. Sometimes I think photographs and films are more powerful than words. Pictures of ordinary, everyday people in pain. Sadly, though, so much of what the outside world sees is politicians posturing. So rarely is the camera there, on the spot, to witness ordinary human suffering.'

Lev liked her. She looked weary. She believed she was a failure after so many years of trying so hard.

'You'll be coming back to Nablus after you've been to your friend's village?'

'I will.'

'I'll see you again then. Good. I'll be here for quite a few more days yet. I want to spend some time in Balata. The refugee camp? You've not heard of it?'

Lev shook his head.

'Ah well. You have now. They say the tanks run through there every day. I want to see for myself. Witnessing, Lev, witnessing, that's what it is all about. We are insignificant aren't we, we foreigners, each of us, individually? It would be better if there were lots of us marching around, wouldn't it? But even singly we can quite often make a difference. The Israelis don't like us to see them shooting at people. If someone foreign is watching, sometimes they hesitate. One hesitation may mean one life saved, one less body maimed. I don't know of any better day's work.'

She put her head between her hands and drifted into silence.

'I'm tired now Lev. These days I feel almost permanently sad. I sometimes think there is nothing more tiring than sadness. Even grief can invigorate on occasions.' She raised a smile. 'See you when you get back. Be sure to find me.'

'If you'd like me to.'

'I would. Have a good trip. Be careful.'

\* \* \*

Lev got directions to Waseem's village from the hotel's recep-
tionist.

'North towards Jenin and west from Anapta towards
Tulkarem.'

The checkpoint was not like those Lev had seen before.
To begin with it was in the middle of a quarry. Trucks full of
stone and grit came and went, making everything dusty and
creating a continual rumble, at times earsplitting. In the
centre of a circular clearing was a concrete cylinder with
horizontal spy slits just beneath a flat concrete cap. The
watchtowers everywhere else looked flimsy and vulnerable;
this specimen was anything but.

There were the usual queues of pedestrians and vehicles
but everything was moving quite smoothly and after forty-five
minutes he was through and looking around for transpor-
tation to Anapta. He had been told he would have to walk
from there. There were minibuses, but the main service to
Anapta was a full-size coach. Every seat was taken.

The route out of Nablus was along a flat road, through
hills and olive trees. The atmosphere in the coach was peaceful and gentle, matching the passing countryside. Passengers
were quietly talking, the old were dozing, children were playing, the sun was warm through the windows. Lev felt more
relaxed than he had done at any time since leaving Rehavia,
but just as he was beginning to doze off himself, the coach
braked sharply and everyone around him instantly became
tense; there was silence. The driver got up, opened the coach
door and got out. Lev heard raised voices, harsh and near-
hysterical.

'Soldiers. Soldiers. There are soldiers.' The whisper came
back from the front of the coach.

The driver reappeared and walked slowly down the aisle between the seats, asking passengers for their identity cards. It took time. People rustled among bags, searched pockets, children whimpered uncertainly, sensing their parents' anxiety. At last, with both hands full, the driver disappeared down the coach steps for a second time. He had looked hard at Lev as he had taken his passport, and Lev had dropped his eyes; he had been identified again. He didn't know whether or not the presence of a Jew on board might make things more complicated for the driver.

After a few minutes the driver appeared again, and told them they had to get out and form a line. The coach was parked on a stretch of road beside a derelict single-storey building. What it had once been used for was not clear. Its windows were blown out, its doors hanging off their hinges. Lev expected to see a whole troop of soldiers, but when he climbed down the coach steps he saw there were just two.

One was prancing around in the deep porch of the abandoned building. It looked as though it may have once been some sort of loading bay. Thin and pale with bad acne, the boy was behaving like he was mounting some sort of last-ditch defence, his back against the wall as if he was sheltering from a barrage of bullets. His behaviour could have been a parody of any Hollywood war film – comic, were he not holding an M16 and pointing it at the passengers as they shambled themselves into a queue beside the coach. His mimicry was as stupid, and just as precise, as the young Arab Lev had watched at Jaffa Gate.

The other soldier was a strapping thug of a boy, broad-shouldered and muscular. He was darting nervously from one spot to another shouting orders, his voice hoarse with the desperate insistence that they should all do as they were told. As the passengers slowly disembarked he seemed surprised – and not a little frightened – to see so many .

He attempted to assert his authority. The crowd was to separate itself into two columns – women and children in one, and men in the other, but they were slow to understand what he was asking them to do; his Arabic was very basic. There was also some reluctance to obey him. He waved his weapon at them; some of the younger men around Lev were muttering to each other, shifting, shuffling, becoming murmuringly restive. The fragility of the soldiers' control over what was happening was all of a sudden apparent. Lev was frightened for his own safety. The atmosphere on this deserted road was volatile, precariously balanced, on the edge of disorder. The soldiers appeared to sense this too and their agitation increased. The pale boy in the porch nervously ranged his rifle over the passengers while the thug's voice rose to a strangled squeak. His instinct, though, was sound: he cleared the ground, ordering the column of women and children back on the coach.

One of the older women was courageous enough to ask for their ID cards back. Both boys looked suddenly fazed by the request. The soldier in the porch nervously slapped the thigh pocket of his uniform. It seemed he had the women's ID cards. For some reason he didn't appear to want to move from where he was, so the other soldier backed off towards him, keeping his gun carefully trained on the passengers, and grabbed them. Scampering quickly back, he gave them to the woman who slowly counted them, deliberately taking her time, lifting her head occasionally to look up at him contemptuously.

He took the men's ID cards out of his pocket, dropping a couple on the ground. Hastily jerking down on to his knees to retrieve them, he dropped some others. After he had finally succeeded in collecting them all up, he piled them on a little wall and picked up the top one. He then called the men towards him by name. As they approached he checked photographs against faces. He told all the older men to get back on the coach but sent the younger men into the porch, where the other soldier herded them into a corner.

When faced with Lev he was clearly surprised, his alarm perhaps betraying the aimless nature of what he and the other soldier were up to. Had they thought they were just going to have a bit of fun, play a game, unwatched by anyone likely to object or restrain them? And now, suddenly, who exactly was this? Reading Lev's passport, he began to look round nervously; he was uncertain. Lev helped him out, speaking in Hebrew.

'Don't worry. None of this is to do with me. I'm a tourist. I'm just passing through. I'm going to Tulkarem. If you give me back my passport, I shall get back on the coach.'

'Yes, alright.'

Returning Lev's passport to him, he tried lamely to claim back some authority.

'You can get on the coach now. Do you hear?'

'Thanks.'

One by one, the other older men slowly followed Lev up the steps of the coach. Suddenly everything had become manageable; the atmosphere lightened. The soldiers relaxed a little, as did the passengers who were back in their seats.

The two soldiers now turned their attention to the six young men who had been told to go and stand in the porch. They were prowling, hands in pockets, shoulders hunched, eyes flashing out hard glances at their captors.

Firstly the soldiers made them stand in a line; then, one by one, they told them to expose their midriffs and lift the bottoms of their trousers to show they had nothing stuck in their shoes. None of them, it appeared, wore socks; their bony ankles somehow diminished their defiance. The first three who were ordered to perform this pantomime complied and were sent back to the coach, wrapping their coats tightly and comfortingly around themselves as they went. The fourth though was told in addition to lean forward against the wall and spread his legs. He was surprised but slowly he did as he was told, bowing his head and resting it against the peeling plaster. The soldier with the acne then began to run his rifle barrel up and down the inside of the young man's legs, nudging the muzzle sharply up into his groin.

It was one indignity too far.

Suddenly the young Arab kicked out and turned on the two soldiers, his fists up. The two soldiers sprang back and brought their rifles to their shoulders.

Shocked at how quickly events had turned from routine to crisis, all those watching through the coach window held their breath. The tension between the three protagonists held them tableau-like, isolated from those looking on, for what seemed minutes but could only have been a second or two. No more than children all three of them, it was a playground confrontation over a football, a standoff over who was top dog, an eye-ball about a girl. Except that the two bullies had guns and the consequence could be far more than a bloody nose or two.

A very remarkable thing then happened.

One of the two Arab boys still waiting to be searched stepped forward and placed himself between the potential combatants. Facing the two young Israelis at arm's length, holding their eyes steadily, he began to talk. He seemed to be appealing to them to back off. He raised both his hands up in front of his chest, his palms forward and apart. As he talked he held his body erect and still. He appeared very calm. The two soldiers were listening intently, and after a few minutes they slowly began to lower their weapons. Reassured that he was making headway, the Arab boy in turn dropped both his hands very gradually and very deliberately to his sides. Continuing to talk and never allowing his gaze to wander from their faces, he then put out his right hand. He was asking for the ID cards to be returned to him. Hesitating, the young thug looked around at his fellow soldier, whose face was expressionless. He looked back, looked around, looked back again at the tall figure in front of him. The young man was still standing there just a metre away; he hadn't so much as twitched a muscle, nor had he withdrawn his hand. The soldier was still undecided. The young Arab raised his chin gently, stretching the curve of his neck into a straight line. It was a subtle gesture of authority. He whispered a few more words. The young soldier inclined his head towards him, to catch the sound of his voice. Hesitantly, he picked the three ID cards up from the floor where they had fallen, put them into the outstretched palm and turned away to face the wall. He wanted it over. He wanted it finished. He was a bully unused to losing.

Confident that he held the moment, the brave young man, with a flick of his shoulders, led the two remaining Arab boys back to the coach, standing at the bottom of the coach steps while they climbed on. Climbing on himself he slammed the door and instructed the driver to drive away. He calmly looked down the coach. In his expression was the command to everyone to settle down and be quiet. Everyone obeyed without question. It was quite a good few minutes before the passengers erupted and started clapping. He was, by then, sitting in his seat trembling, oblivious of the noise around him.

Soon, everyone lapsed into a relieved silence.

Lev knew that something very tragic had almost happened.

\* \* \*

After ten minutes a barrier came into view. No one on the coach seemed surprised; they just got out, walked round it and went looking for a minibus on the other side to take them onwards. There were four or five parked waiting. One was to Anapta; Lev jumped in and was asked for a shekel; it could not be far. Arriving within ten minutes Lev got out and asked directions. The main road, a shuttered shop and a mean little stall selling a few tired looking vegetables seemed to be all there was to this drab settlement. There were very few people around. Some men, sitting disconsolately on the steps of a nondescript mosque, watched Lev, without seeing him.

After a long trek uphill and several enquiries to reassure himself he was going in the right direction, Lev found himself walking up a rough track beside a plastered stone wall too high for him to see over. He knocked on a little iron door. There was no answer. He waited and knocked again. Still no answer. He pushed at the door and it gave. He found he was looking into a yard. There was a man dozing in a white plastic chair just inside the threshold of a set of double doors at the top of a little set of steps. Lev didn't quite know what to do, so he cleared his throat loudly, waking Waseem's uncle Fahmi with a start.

Waseem and his uncle lived in a house on a hillside overlooking a little valley crowded with other similar houses. Most had a small yard angled to catch the warm early morning sun and to lose it when it became too hot, with an olive tree and perhaps an almond tree. Fahmi Ibrahim's yard also had a lemon tree, as well as an outside squat toilet and a little lean-to shed where the sheep were kept in semi-darkness, the ram stamping in a separate pen. Their house, like all the others, was constructed quite simply: a concrete frame filled with breezeblocks, the off-white walls lightly plastered.

In Fahmi's house there was a large public room, about five metres square, where guests were entertained, and family photographs and framed certificates were on view. In this room, too, was a gilt-framed, panoramic photograph of the Grand Mosque in Mecca with the Ka'aba floodlit in the centre and thousands of pilgrims in white robes circling it. There were also some framed texts from the Koran. It was furnished with a number of sofas set around the walls, rugs and carpets on the floor and lots of little tables. There was a family room, slightly smaller than the public room, with floor cushions and mattresses. Next to the family room was the kitchen, which was smaller again. The ceilings were all quite low, no more than half a metre above head height. The bedroom was as large as the public room, though rectangular rather than square, with a huge double bed slept in by Fahmi. The bedroom was also where the family's clothes were kept, in two small wardrobes. Everyone else slept either on mattresses on the family-room floor, or in the dining room. Lev had his bed made up for him on the floor of the public room among the sofas. The house had no heating except for a small low brazier on wheels, kept in the family room.

To begin with it was very difficult. Nobody had heard from Jack and, until Lev turned up, it was assumed he was on his way. Waseem was especially disappointed to find out that his brother wouldn't be coming after all. They were also, quite naturally, suspicious of this very obviously Jewish man suddenly in their house, although it was never openly mentioned by either of them. Lev had told them he was Jack's friend and both appeared to take that at face value, although it must have been clear to them quite soon that he actually knew very little about Jack. Waseem wanted to know a lot about his brother and at the outset asked a lot of questions. Lev was embarrassed by how little he could tell him, and Waseem soon gave up asking. He and his uncle could not have been blamed for wondering what Lev was really doing in their house. Their discomfort never quite disappeared during his brief stay, although they made great efforts to make him feel welcome and, within their strait-ened means, to make him comfortable.

Waseem had come back soon after Lev arrived. In appearance he was quite similar to his brother, but was calmer and less challenging. Fahmi bore no physical resem-blance to either of them: he was tall, very thin and almost bald. His sallow face was hung with creases and he had a blank eye – the result of a bullet ricochet during a distur-bance many years before, when he had been away working in Israel. From a medical point of view, Lev thought he might be quite unwell, perhaps even in constant pain. If that was the case, he wasn't letting on. It turned out that he was the same age as Udi, although he looked much older, and spent a substantial part of each day in a chair dozing.

He was unfailingly courteous, but spoke very little. He obviously listened intently to everything that was said around him. Lev had casually mentioned to Waseem that he hadn't yet eaten kanafe during this trip but remembered it as being deliciously sweet. It was served the following day at the end of the evening meal, Fahmi having gone out to buy some specially that morning.

Fahmi and Waseem were looked after by Fahmi's only daughter. Lev caught only very brief glimpses of her and was never introduced. During his four days in Fahmi's house he never even learnt her name. She spent her time either in the kitchen, the bedroom or the family room, and elaborate manoeuvres were undertaken to ensure Lev didn't come face to face with her. He was never left alone except when he went to bed. The only route into the house was via the family room, through which Lev was always ushered quickly to the dining room or public room. When she had to lay the table for the three of them to eat, the door from the public room into the dining room was shut. When she was in the family room or in the kitchen cooking, the other dining room door was shut. Fahmi's daughter was never referred to at any time, although her presence was palpable.

Lev had noticed a satellite dish on the roof, and one evening asked if he could watch BBC World on the television. However, he couldn't relax while watching, knowing she must be either hanging around somewhere out of sight – in the kitchen perhaps, or twiddling her thumbs, sitting on the bed in the main bedroom. No mention was made of a husband or children, and Lev guessed she had neither. There were certainly no photographs of any small children anywhere. The only photograph of someone whom he thought might be her showed a young woman in a group, her face partly obscured by the arm of the woman next to her. There were balloons in the background. Likewise, there was only one photograph of Jack. It had been taken recently and he was in tennis gear.

Lev spent most of his time with Waseem. On one occasion, he accompanied Fahmi up the hill to the mosque, waiting outside for him while he went in to pray, but Lev felt that he was agitated by his presence. Lev and Waseem sat in the yard a great deal, fed the sheep, walked in the fields with Waseem's donkey, and tended the bees that belonged to a cousin who lived in Tulkarem.

Every evening, the three of them sat in the public room and friends from the village called by to meet the visitor. Lev could manage quite challenging conversations in Arabic now, and handled many such conversations during those evenings in the public room. Every evening, too, the electricity was cut for an hour, something to do with grid overload. Battery-powered lamps were kept in the cupboard in readiness.

The conversation was sometimes about Jack but more often about 'the situation'. The village's primary school teacher had been the first to bring it up. When it was clear that the subject did not embarrass Lev the conversation became freer, more animated. Lev did not attempt to hide his Jewishness. He prevaricated instead.

'I feel very English now, having lived in London for so many years. It's not how I remember it here. Not how it was when I was young. It appears to have changed a great deal.'

Most of all though they wanted to tell him about the soldiers.

'One man was shot in his car going between his home in the village and his work in Anapta, just last week. His brother was shot in similar circumstances a year ago.'

'Was the family suspected of something?'

'If they were, then we didn't know why. We all know the family well. We would have known if they had anything to do with the resistance.'

'These shootings are random, Lev, wanton; possibly it was just target practice.'

'On both occasions?'

'Why not? In Nablus most evenings the soldiers shoot down on the Old City from the camp on the hill.'

'Why?'

'To remind us they're there? For fun? Who knows? They're probably very bored.'

'I didn't hear anything when I was there.'

'When were you there?'

Lev told them.

'That night there were tanks in the main street of the bazaar. A dozen people were arrested. You didn't see or hear any of that, either.'

They told him too about the armoured cars in the streets of their village, especially after dark, and of the tanks that ripped up the roads, of the burning down of factories and the random destruction of water pipes, sewers and houses. They were very anxious to make it clear, however, that these events had happened at various times over the last four or five years, that they hadn't happened all at once and didn't happen every day; there could be months with no incidents. But they were never sure when something might happen and, when something did happen, what had prompted it. Their lives were clouded permanently by uncertainty. The soldiers were a feared presence.

There were other factors at play here: the soldiers' apparent unaccountability, the completely free hand they seemed to have to behave pretty much as they liked. Soldiers so young they had yet to decide on their own behavioural boundaries were given weapons and uniforms and then sent out into these remote valleys, far from their homes. It was a dangerous project for the young Israelis and the Palestinian people alike.

Every night Lev opened the windows of his room and went to sleep to the sounds of bleating sheep and braying donkeys.

＊　＊　＊

Even after centuries, the landscape surrounding Fahmi's village barely tolerated the people who farmed and lived off it. The hills were rock-strewn and steeply sloping; the olive trees – some of which, Waseem told him, had been there since Roman times – were planted only where they could be accommodated. Patches of ground had been painstakingly cleared of rocks, which had then been used to build the low walls that surrounded them. Their builders respected the land's contours and irregularities, detouring around any boulder or rocky outcrop that proved too difficult to move. Despite the meticulous clearance, there still remained a patina of white reflective gravel, protecting the fertile soil beneath from the unrelenting sun that shone for nine months of each year.

Among the olive trees were wild almond trees and native oaks. It was the leaves of the almond trees that were the reason for the expedition this afternoon. Waseem needed to collect a sack-full to feed his sheep. He had bought a new saddle for his donkey but it was still hard so he only rode the animal for short periods so as to not chafe its back.

Hidden among the grass and wildflowers were wells; some had dried up and, Wassim said, had become the homes of snakes. The new wells were topped with small blocks of concrete so that they could be located easily. Bolted into the concrete were hinged metal flaps to prevent the wells from being polluted by wildlife – Waseem explained that there were wild cats and foxes; there were certainly moles, little mounds of moist earth were everywhere. Attached to the hinged flaps were lengths of rope tied to small metal buckets to bring up the water. Although it was mid afternoon, they soon became sweaty and dusty, so washed themselves. The water was cool, clear and soft, and tasted very clean.

Where the almond trees grew was an hour's walk from the village. Some of the route was along the highway to Tulkarem. They dipped off after a few metres down a slope and walked the remainder of the way along a roadway between drystone walls which had been repaired in places, the new stone white and free of moss and lichen. Like the walls around the olive trees the path they were taking wound its way over the undulating landscape, following natural contours and avoiding steep slopes. It was roughly paved and bright green grass grew from between the stones. As Lev and Waseem entered the oval bowl of the valley where Fahmi's fields were, Lev could see, in the distance, an intricate network of similar paths between the fields of olive trees. They looked as if they had been there forever.

Fahmi's village had now entirely disappeared from view. They were in a lovely, lonely place. It was clear to Lev, sitting there peacefully, why the Israelis wanted it so badly and the Palestinians wanted so much to hang on to it.

He sat on a flat rock while Waseem hacked off whole branches from the almond trees. The sun was beginning to drop behind a ridge of low hills to the west and the scenery took on a mellow golden glow, softening the bright whiteness of the earlier afternoon, making the place even more paradisal. An owl hooted. In the full heat of the summer that whiteness might look very harsh, even forbidding; this afternoon it was just perfect.

Slowly, though, as shadows lengthened and light and shade became more distinct, there appeared on the top of the hill behind him silhouettes of some single-storey buildings and a water tower on four thin supports; stark against the deep blue sky.

'Waseem, who lives up there? Why should people want to live up there?'

'Up there? They're not people. They're soldiers.'

Waseem laughed at his unintended joke.

He explained that on the other side of the hill to their right was an old Jewish pioneer settlement that had been there for more than twenty years, but that last year a new settlement was begun over the hill to their left. The government had decided that both settlements needed protection, and the military camp had then been built. Waseem pointed further up the hill towards the camp.

'Those there were our fields too, but the soldiers took

them and they took other fields as well, belonging to people in the next village, on the other side of the hill.'

'Why?'

'Security.'

'Security?'

'We can't go.'

'How much have they taken?'

Waseem drew a triangle on the ground with the end of a stick. He put three stones inside the triangle to indicate the settlements and the camp and then another larger one to indicate Tulkarem, to give some idea of scale. He also traced a road which he said went from his cousin's village to Tulkarem.

'This road is now closed to us. It is an Israeli road. My cousin has to come through our village now, if he wants to go to his family's home.'

'But that's miles longer.'

'Double the distance. Yes.'

'And this area you've marked out here is huge. How many fields have you lost?'

'Three.'

'But you've only got five.'

'We had eight. My cousin's father in law has lost six. He now has only four.'

'And your income?'

'Much less of course.'

Lev looked up at the camp. Waseem smiled at him.

'Even here we are watched.'

He shrugged.

'Back now?'

A chill breeze had sprung up. Lev was cold and the route

back felt arduous. The stony ground of the ancient roadway to the Tulkarem highway now seemed difficult, every stone sharp through the soles of his shoes, every irregularity jarring his body. Even the beautiful blue sky seemed to have lost its lustre. Not for the first time since he left Rehavia, Lev was shivering.

\* \* \*

The next morning Waseem walked him down to Anapta. Earlier, Fahmi had organised for a friend to come by to take a photograph of the three of them beside the lemon tree. Lev was greatly touched.

Sitting on a bank in the sun, beside the yellow iron barrier outside Anapta, waiting for the bus to Nablus to turn up, Lev was very aware of the tranquillity he felt. He had felt it the afternoon before, too, until he had seen the military camp up on the hill. It was a strange tranquillity, intense rather than serene. He could feel it pressing in on him, demanding attention. The tranquillity of these gentle hills, these rock-studded slopes and the olive trees that covered them was not the caressing tranquillity of an English summer day but a vibrant, vital tranquillity that excited rather than soothed.

Lev sipped the coffee he had bought from a temporary stall. He looked up the hill opposite, through the rocks and olive trees to the top, and there, its solar panels and water tank sharp against the sky, was another military camp. 'Even here we are watched,' Waseem had said, and on this tranquil road outside Anapta, peacefully sipping their coffee in the sun, they were being spied on as well.

\* \* \*

Back in Nablus, Lev went straight to the hotel, dumped his bags and went out.

He needed something to eat and looked for somewhere to get a quick shwarma. Standing at a counter, he felt a gentle tap on his arm.

"Friends. There your friends." It was the woman behind him in the queue.

Peering into the back of the café he saw Margarette and Omar sitting at a tiny round table. They were beckoning him to come over.

'You know each other?' said Lev.

'Of course. How do you think I get into Nablus – fly? Omar arranges everything. He's always at the checkpoint near Hawara. What are you doing now?'

'I was going to have a look round Nablus.'

'Do you want a guide?'

'Well I hadn't thought about it.'

'Omar's your man. Go with Omar. He'll show you everything. He knows where to get the best kanafe too.'

'Thanks. I'd like that. If it's alright with you, Omar?'

'Of course it is. Omar would love to.'

He winked.

'Omar, are you sure?'

'I'm sure, Lev.'

'And another thing. I've some people coming to the hotel tonight at about eight. Please come. On the bridge. You know where?'

'Yes I do. Thanks.'

'See you then. Eight sharp. Have a good time. There is much to see. Don't wear him out Omar!' Margarette affectionately tapped Omar on his arm. 'Bring him back safely.'

'He'll be safe with me.'

Omar took Lev first to the site of what was once a large two-storey building.

'The building that used to be here was a thousand years old; built as a night shelter for traders on the camel route between the Mediterranean and central Syria. You understand me?'

'Perfectly. A caravanserai is what you mean.'

'Yes. A caravanserai. That's it.'

'But it's a wreck.'

'Yes, now a ruin.'

Only three walls remained. It had been converted long ago into a covered market. One or two little arched cavities, where shops must have been, were still fraily intact. The flattened space in the middle was as large as a tennis court. Most of the rubble had been cleared away, leaving it desolate and empty. Backing on to the old caravanserai was another demolished building; none of its walls remained. Another blank space was all that was left.

'That was a soap factory. Nablus soap is famous for its purity. It has been made in Nablus for centuries.'

'I know, Omar. My brother and I used to come up here and buy it for our mother, when we were students. I seemed to remember that this place was where we used to go.'

'It was the biggest factory and the oldest. There are others. You can still buy Nablus soap. Before you leave, I'll show you where, if you like. There's one not far from your hotel.'

'What happened here?'

'Israeli rockets, one night two years ago.'

'Why?'

'The Israelis say they are looking for terrorists. And the rest of the world believes them.'

'All this damage in one night?'

'Just one night.'

Omar led Lev down into the Old City. Although the tangle of lanes and alleys resembled Old City Jerusalem, the streets of Old Nablus were in many places entirely covered. Arch after arch after arch stretched into the distance down every alley and lane. Some of the streets were so dark that Omar and Lev had to feel their way; sometimes they stumbled. There were light fixtures fitted into the ancient brickwork above their heads but none were working.

Through an open doorway they saw an octagonal pool in a decorated alcove, typically Islamic in design and made of orange and black marble, the fountain at its centre still bubbling. The house had once been very grand. There was no roof beyond the deep porch and no interior walls either. The great wooden door had been split in two. One half was leaning against a wall and the other lay scattered in pieces on the ground.

'Still looking for terrorists?'

'That's what they say.'

Omar then took Lev along a cobbled lane where, in between otherwise intact houses and shops, were heaps of rubbish and shattered masonry, broken tiles and exposed electrical wiring. The destruction had been precise. Single buildings had been targeted and destroyed. Like a smile from which individual teeth had been smashed rather than drawn.

'This was my father-in-law's house.'

Omar had stopped at a rubble-filled site between two shops, where a modest two-storey dwelling had clearly once stood. The marks of a staircase were still visible on the back wall.

'Was he killed?'

'No but my wife's sister and her baby daughter were.'

'I'm so sorry.'

Omar barely acknowledged what Lev said. He was look-ing at what had once been his wife's childhood home with tears in his eyes.

'Where does he live now?'

'Who?'

'Your father-in-law.'

'With me.'

'And your mother in law?'

'She died three months after the attack.'

'Why? Because of this?'

'She just gave up, Lev.'

Omar led Lev out of town.

'We'll go back and have a look at the bazaar and the old mosque later, if that's alright?'

'I'm in your hands.'

'There is just one more place I want to show you. The rest you can see for yourself as we walk. It's all around us, the wreckage.'

And Omar was right. As they walked, they rarely passed a row of more than two or three buildings together without some major damage: roofs and walls demolished, front doors kicked in and windows shattered. Walking was diffi-cult because hardly any pavements were undamaged; heaps of shattered masonry were everywhere and the roads were mostly ripped up.

'No wonder the soldiers stop tourists coming here.'

They were on the outskirts of the town now.

'There. Just take a look at that!'

'What was it?'

'It was the Palestinian Authority's main administration headquarters for the Nablus area. It was built originally by you British. The Israelis tell the world that they are allowing us to govern ourselves; then they smash up our means of doing so and say to the world, "See, we told you they were incapable of it."'

Omar's voice was not so much bitter as weary and resigned.

Before them was a scene of devastation.

The flat-roofed building had once been four storeys tall. Each floor had been split, smashed or buckled by a succession of upended swathes of concrete, which slanted diagonally from above roof level to its cellars. The building looked as though it had been picked up by some giant hand and dropped, not just once, but several times. Huge lumps of masonry dangled like the carcasses of meat Lev had seen in the bazaar in Jerusalem. The outside walls were almost entirely blown out. Great dark cavities had been formed, some two or even three storeys high, and they were crammed with twisted metal girders and concrete pillars snapped in half like matchsticks. The contents of the different rooms were so comprehensively damaged and destroyed that they almost defied identification. Lev could just make out the remains of filing cabinets, desks and tables. To have described what was left as a shell would have been inaccurate, just as it would have been to have described it as a skeleton – too little remained intact. Yet it stood defiant, a congealing ruin, made more shocking because it was still in one wrecked piece, and on such a colossal scale.

'Enough?'

'Enough.'

Back in the bazaar, Lev dutifully looked at what was left of the delicate tracery over the door to the Friday Mosque, peered in through a window at the prayer hall and the Roman pillars supporting it, and let Omar treat him to some kanafe. But he was surfeited, he had seen more than enough; he wanted to go back to his hotel.

'Nablus was once so lovely,' he said.

'I have a report at home, written more than ten years ago by some tourist consultants from Norway. They identified a number of unique and historical buildings and places in Nablus Old City around which we could develop a flourishing tourist trade. All are now destroyed. You understand me?'

'Yes, Omar, perfectly.'

'You're tired now, I can see. So I'll show you where you buy soap and then get you back. You have an appointment with Margarette tonight I think?'

'I have. Thanks, Omar. Thanks for everything.'

Returning to his room, Lev showered the dust of the wrecked city away. He still had two hours before he was due to meet Margarette and her friends. He set his alarm and took a nap.

* * *

The hotel occupied two separate buildings, the lobby in one and the guests' rooms in the other. The bridge where Margarette had told him to meet her joined the buildings at the first floor level. It was wide and had floor-to-ceiling windows on either side from which guests could watch the busy bazaar below while eating. There was a restaurant next to the lobby but eating on the bridge was much nicer, and much more private. Lev got dressed and wandered down the corridor from his room. As he approached the double doors that opened on to the bridge, he could hear talking. It was Margarette's voice.

'Everyone knows that the world's media is much more likely to be interested in running a story if a foreigner's involved. A Palestinian getting hurt at a checkpoint is no-where near as newsworthy.'

She was deep in conversation with an athletic-looking young man wearing a tight red t-shirt, and a woman who was sitting with her back towards Lev as he came through the doors. Margarette glanced up at Lev and said some-thing to her companions. The man immediately jumped nimbly to his feet. The woman, dressed in an expensive cream silk blouse, instead of getting up, twisted slowly round in her chair, tilting her head to look up at him.

'Emile, this is Lev Dubnow. Lev, meet Emile Delaunay.'

As Lev was about to shake Delaunay's hand, he suddenly recognised the woman looking up at him.

'Rachel? What are you doing here?'

## 4. Nablus Checkpoint

'The worst that can happen to you, Lev, is that you get deported.'

'Do I really want to get deported?'

'Hawara would be better of course but it's much too open.'

'Hawara? Nobody's mentioned Hawara before.'

'It's the checkpoint to the south of Nablus on the road to Ramallah,' said Margarette. 'For our purposes it would be far too exposed. There would be nowhere for you to hide yourself and your equipment, Emile. It's like Qalandia, cleared ground all around. The checkpoint on the road to Anapta is crowded and has this quarry where trucks come and go all the time. There's a steep hillside with bushes and trees to one side of it. In other words, lots of cover.'

'And anyway,' said Rachel, 'doesn't Omar know someone important at the quarry?'

'He does.'

'Who doesn't Omar know?' said Emile Delaunay.

'Margarette, if I get deported I'll never be able to return, will I?'

'No, Lev, you won't.'

'Not unless what we are fighting for here comes to pass and there's a change,' said Emile.

'Then you'll be a hero and you'll be very welcome here.'

'Won't the dust from the quarry be a problem?' asked Rachel.

'Omar reckons he can stop the trucks coming in and out of it for as much as ten minutes,' said Margarette.

'Is that enough?'

'Should be, but can he be relied upon?' asked Emile.

'Who?'

'This Omar.'

'Absolutely.'

'Who is he exactly?'

'An old and very dear friend of mine. And someone who looks for all the world like an Israeli border guard except that he smiles and hasn't the capacity to be unpleasant to anybody if he tried. Is it settled then?'

Rachel looked around at them all.

'Emile?'

'Everything seems fine to me.'

'Lev?'

'Yes fine. I'll do it. Don't worry.'

Margarette leant across and lightly touched his arm.

'Thanks, Lev.'

\* \* \*

Checking out of his hotel the next morning, Lev crossed the street and went into one of the few of Nablus' famous soap factories that still remained. Bars of soap wrapped in white tissue paper were heaped around its walls waiting to be bought. The cavernous place was completely empty except for three workers, who all jumped up to serve him when he entered. He bought some soap for Sarah as he had promised. A dozen little cubes were dropped into a small black plastic bag which he tied to the handle of his own bag.

Out again in the sun he glanced at his watch. 10.30. The sky was cloudless. He had time.

Rachel had been tight-lipped over breakfast. The news had just come through of a bus bombing outside a supermarket in the district where she lived in West Jerusalem. Ten had died, three were critical and fifty were injured.

'The possibility of friends?'

'High.'

'Relatives?'

'Just as high.'

'Do you never have any doubts, Rachel, about getting involved in the way you are?'

'Of course I have, Lev, all the time. What do you think? But then …'

'But then?'

'I have to force myself to remember the inequity. Around the world it is beamed: ten Israelis dead. A cowardly act of cold-blooded slaughter. Suicide bombers strike again. We Israelis don't need to use suicide bombers, we have F16 rockets. Do you know how many were killed in Gaza this week alone? The same number. Did you know that?'

'No.'

'I thought not. Well at least you know now. And all that was needed to murder and maim so many was one rocket. Just one. Nobody risks their lives killing Palestinians.'

'Tit for tat?'

'Isn't it always? But does anyone give a thought to how everyday, ordinary Palestinians feel when they hear the news?

They groan, that's what they do; they groan, they shrug, they become just a little wearier. Longer queues at checkpoints, more intimate body searches, more buses stopped at random. And ordinary, everyday Israelis, don't you think they groan too? Trust me Lev, that's exactly what they do. They may become a little more frightened, a little more bewildered and some too will even become a little more hardline, but they will groan just the same. Another hour going to work this morning, the Arab shop on the corner that sells the lovely, fresh falafel will probably be closed today again. That's not how it's depicted though is it? No, the immediate reaction is always supposed to be revenge, retribution. I don't believe that. I believe that the immediate response of most ordinary, everyday people, Palestinian and Israeli, is not of revenge but of weary resignation, "Not again, not again, when will this ever end?" The outside world never hears from them though, does it? It only hears the indignant clatter of posturing politicians. I sometimes think that the politicians, of both sides, actually thrive on conflict and revenge, would shrivel without it.'

'Politicians get targeted too.'

'Of course they do. Tell me though, Lev, how many are seen on the street alone without being surrounded by security?'

'The few I've seen have all been in cars.'

Rachel looked down at her hands thoughtfully.

'Were there any politicians at that funeral you went to in Ramallah?'

'Not that I saw.'

'No, of course there weren't. The rain would have spoilt the creases in their damn trousers.'

'Hamas was there in force.'

'Of course it was. Is it any wonder, then, the high regard in which it's held?'

'They were only kids though, Rachel.'

'At least *someone* from Hamas was there, Lev, kids or not. The point is, if there had been a few well-known faces there, even if there had been only one, then there just might have been a TV camera from some European or US news agency there too. And that shocking poster of the little nine year old might just have been seen by someone outside Ramallah. That's why it's up to people like us to bring the misery and weariness of the ordinary people to the attention of those outside. That's why we are resorting to taking our own photographs and shooting our own film, in the hope that someone, somewhere will eventually say this can't be allowed to continue, this has got to end. Just one stark image can have such an effect. It has happened before.'

'I do understand, you know.'

'I hope so, because what we have planned for Nablus Checkpoint today is asking a lot from you and may end very badly for you too. You should know how grateful we are.'

'Rachel, can I ask you something?'

'What's that Lev?'

'How did you, of all people, get involved in all this?'

'You mean "why?" don't you Lev, not "how?" It's easy enough to get involved.'

'OK. Why?'

'I've had enough, Lev. Our problem is that we can't stop seeing ourselves as victims.'

'With some justification. What about the bus bombing in Jerusalem this morning?'

'It must have been just awful but there are surprisingly few incidents, if you consider what we do to the Palestinians every day of the week. And we only get away with that because of the world's conscience about what happened to us.'

'But the Holocaust shouldn't be forgotten.'

'It's the horror of it that shouldn't be forgotten. You must remember those old black and white films of Jews being herded off to the death camps carrying their suitcases.'

'As if they were going on holiday.'

'We were shown them endlessly as children, weren't we?'

'We were.'

'Yet the emphasis was never on the horror of it all. The lesson we were told we should learn from those films was that it was us against the world. The world against us. I love this country dearly, and I want to stay here, live here, help it grow and flourish. But our leaders persist in waging war – a war that is unequal, unjust and unnecessary, an old man's war. Our leaders, Jewish and Arab alike, are such old men Lev. They have been fighting all their lives and they know little else.'

She sighed.

'They say on the West Bank, "Not until the old men die."'

'I've heard it more than once.'

'But they have such resilience, these old boys: heart conditions, raging diabetes, weight problems, yet there they still are, spreading their poison. I'm not getting any younger Lev; I can't wait for them all to die off one by one. I want to have children but I don't want any children of mine brought up here as it is at the moment. Nor do I want any more of my friends' children becoming soldiers and having their optimism knocked out of them, their aspirations and ambitions damaged and distorted by fear. There's no Mandela figure among those myopic old men, to lead us out of this swamp. As far as I can see there will have to be an intervention from outside. And that's what we're about Lev Dubnow: trying to convince someone, somewhere, that enough is enough, that something must be done. Guaranteeing fair borders for a generation would be a start.'

'It's not complicated, is it?'

'No, Lev, it's not. It's about drawing a line, that all.'

\* \* \*

Lev walked up into the bazaar from the soap factory. Omar had rather rushed him round the previous afternoon so he thought he'd take the opportunity to look more closely at some of the dark, arched lanes that he'd only had a chance to glimpse. He came across a crossroad of arched tunnels where the vaulted roof resembled that of a crusader castle or a Byzantine basilica. The people lived above the thoroughfare and to support the weight of their homes sturdy arches had been constructed, one after another after another. These arched tunnels gave Nablus a mysterious, private atmosphere, as if the action was going on elsewhere – as indeed it was, way above head height.

He found again the bombed out house with the orange and black ornamental pool. Beyond the garden was another house, its plaster and stone first-floor ceiling slanting steeply down because one of the retaining walls had been blown away. Despite the damage, the basic structure of the building had survived. He found some steps, intact and swept. Climbing them he discovered, at second-storey level, a patio with four or five front doors opening on to it, potted plants and washing hanging out to dry. The courtyards of Nablus were in the sky and were fashioned defiantly out of the ruins.

The impression he'd had the day before was that there hadn't been much repair work done, that the rocket damage had just been left as a sort of memorial. As he walked around now though he saw that in fact a lot of work had been undertaken. In some ways the repairs emphasised the extraordinary damage inflicted on Nablus rather than masking it. The work had been done hurriedly and for purely practical reasons, to make dwellings and shops inhabitable.

Lev glanced at his watch. He'd better get a move on. It was a little after 11.30. He looked about for a taxi.

\* \* \*

Getting out of his cab, Lev looked down towards the checkpoint. There was some sort of hold-up. A crowd of about a hundred was squashed into an area of cleared ground little more than six metres wide, between a wire fence and a bank. The fence separated the pedestrian footpath from the road, where long queues of vehicles were waiting, horns sounding and angry voices being raised. The bank was steep but some people scrambled up it, to get free of the crowd or to see exactly what the reason was for the delay. Lev looked up the bank to see if he could pick out Emile. He couldn't. He began then to shoulder his way through the crowd to see for himself what was happening.

As he got closer he saw what the problem was. From the fence to the bank, there was a row of concrete cubes, just like the ones he had seen at Qalandia, and a young soldier was trying to herd everyone back behind them, lunging and jabbing at those in the front of the crowd with the butt of his rifle.

'Behind. Behind. Get behind.'

He was shouting in Hebrew and kicking at the ground, sending dust into people's faces. As they retreated, Lev was pushed back against a concrete block and almost stumbled.

'Hold on. Hold on. Why is he doing this?'

Lev's enquiry was to no one in particular and it was met with shrugs and tired, raised eyebrows.

Predictably, after a few moments, the crowd began slowly to surge forward again under the pressure of newcomers at the back. The soldier reacted viciously again, waving the barrel of his gun in the faces of those unlucky enough to be at the front.

Another, apparently less bellicose, soldier came up. Tall and as slender as the jacaranda saplings around the English lawn at the Allenby Bridge, he was no older than the other soldier – eighteen or nineteen. Trying to take charge, he directed everyone to divide into two groups: woman and children near the fence; men beside the bank. There was anger and confusion as the crowd unwillingly complied.

A voice from behind urged Lev on.

'You go forward. You can go forward.'

He heard other voices too.

'He can go forward. Go on. Go forward. Let him through.'

The first young soldier was leaning against the fence. He was a short, stubby boy, thick-necked, with a crew-cut. His hands were so large as to be immediately noticeable. They were rural hands, hard, gnarled and scarred. He watched the confusion with a smile.

When everything had quietened down, he called a young Arab woman towards him. Her hejab was augmented by a khimer, a silk cloth that covered her nose, mouth and chin. Her eyes, barely visible through the silken slit, flicked across at her husband in the men's group as she approached the soldier. Her husband held a toddler in his arms. The child was watching his mother.

'My husband. My husband must come too.'

'Later.'

She edged forward.

'My husband. My husband must be with me.'

'I told you before. I'll call him later. You first.'

He put out his hand. She flinched.

'ID?'

She fumbled in her bag, found it and gave it to him. He looked down at her card and then back up at her.

'I can't see your face. Lift that cloth.'

He spoke in English but with a New York accent.

She stepped back and stood looking at him. Lev could see her young body tense.

'Lift that cloth.'

She hesitated, fiddled with her fingers, clearly at a loss as to how she should deal with what had been asked of her. She looked back at her husband again. She was plainly frightened.

Lev stepped out from the crowd and spoke in Hebrew.

'You can't do that. She cannot do as you ask. Give her ID back to her. Let her through and her husband and child too.'

The boy slowly turned his shorn head in Lev's direction. His eyes were a piercing blue, his skin pasty.

'And you are?'

'You know what you are asking her to do is unacceptable. You must know that, so why are asking her to lift her khimer? If she does so, you'll have shamed her. In front of all these people. In front of her husband. In front of her son. Is that what you want? Is that what you're after? Why? Why would you want to give her such distress? What would be the good of that to you? Let her through. In fact, why don't you let all these people through, let them all go home. There are old people here who are weary, little children who need to be fed, women with bags.'

Lev had walked up to the young soldier and put himself between him and the frightened young woman.

He proffered his passport. The soldier looked at its cover.

'You are English?'

'I am.'

'Why were you in Nablus?'

'I am a visitor here.'

'We don't allow tourists into Nablus.'

'You don't? Well you allowed me, just yesterday, right here, at this very checkpoint. Your colleagues were too busy playing the fool to check my papers properly. They barely looked at my passport. Slipped up badly there didn't they? I could have been a terrorist. To think Israel depends on people as slipshod as you lot for their safety.'

The young soldier looked inside the passport.

'But you were born in Jerusalem?'

'I was.'

'Then you're a Jew?'

'I am.'

The soldier looked confused.

'Why? Don't you think a Jew could be a terrorist? Do you

really believe all Jews support the sort of thing that's going on here? A lot of us feel the way you kids behave towards these people at checkpoints is outrageous. Can you tell me please why you are holding these people up in the way you are?'

'Orders.'

'Whose orders?'

The boy glanced quickly over his shoulder at a hut which presumably housed the officer in charge. He waved his arm, pointing a finger at Lev.

'She'll be here soon.'

'Don't wait for her, just let them through now. Let them go to their homes. They've been held up long enough already.'

'What's a Jew doing in Nablus? What have you been doing there?'

'I'll tell you what I've been doing. I've been looking at the devastation that's been inflicted on the Old City. I've been looking at the homes that have been destroyed, at the buildings that are wrecked. I've been looking at the posters of the dead. And shall I tell you something? I'm ashamed, deeply ashamed.'

A tiny girl soldier came up, swaggering with insolent self-confidence.

'What's he saying?'

'He's ranting on about Nablus.'

'Oh is he?'

'He has an English passport.'

'So?'

'He's a Jew though.'

'He's one of them then, isn't he? You know, Dan, like we had here last week. Has his bag been checked? What's that dangling from the handle?'

'Soap,' said Lev.

'Soap?'

'Nablus is famous for its soap.'

'Is it really?'

She came up very close to Lev and slowly circled him.

'Why are you standing with these people? They are Arabs. You don't have to wait. Once your bags have been checked you can go through. Do you have a problem with that?'

'The problem, officer, is to do with your colleague. I have been asking him to let these people go through the checkpoint and he adamantly refuses.'

'He's obeying orders.'

'Your orders?'

'My orders. You can go but they must wait, they have to be checked.'

'Well check them then.'

'We are.'

'No you're not. You're keeping them penned like animals in a cage. If your job is to check them then check them and then let them go.'

'When we are ready.'

'No. Not when you're ready. Now.'

'Who are you anyway?'

'You've no right to hold them like this. Let them go.'

'We have every right. We are in control here.'

'Is that right?' Lev looked over at the soldier who had his passport. 'Well, he's had quite enough time to check my passport so I'll have it back, if you don't mind.'

Lev leant across and snatched his passport back.

'Thank you.' He looked down at the young girl officer. 'If you'll stand aside now please?'

'Where do you think you're going?'

'Where do you think? Now step aside.'

But Lev didn't wait for her to move; instead he stepped to her right and walked past her, back towards the waiting crowd. Omar was there, standing at the front, looking straight at him. His eyes flickered encouragement. Lev took a deep breath, dredging his mind for the right colloquial Arabic.

'I've asked the soldiers to allow you all through. I'm sure you'll not be held up anymore.'

'Stop that,' said the girl.

Lev turned and faced the three soldiers. He was trying not to tremble. The soldier who had got the crowd to divide into two groups had his gun at his shoulder and was aiming it at Lev. Lev took a couple of steps in his direction, just enough to put the palm of his outstretched hand on the barrel of the weapon and push it to one side.

'What were you going to do? Eh? Shoot me?'

There was silence, a huge silence. Dust swirled up in the light breeze. Lev could taste it, gritty and salty on his lips. His eyes began to smart.

'And what would you do, young man, if these patient, gentle people here –' Lev gestured towards the crowd '– if these people disregarded you, and tried to walk through this checkpoint despite you and your guns? What if they chose to take their chances? Would you shoot them too? Would your mates in that wretched little pillbox over there mow them down?'

There was another huge silence. Everyone was motionless.

'Well? Is that what would happen? Shall we try it? You never know, they might follow me. Shall I call them all again?'

Lev looked at the three soldiers one by one and shook his head wearily.

'Look at you. You are young enough to be my children. You're frightened aren't you?' He hesitated, lowering his voice. 'Think for a moment. You have an opportunity here. You can stop bullying these people. You can stand aside and let them through. Go on, do it. Just this once.'

Lev looked at the tall slender soldier and held his gaze. The boy's curls were speckled with white stone-yard dust.

'Go on. Let them go, lad. Just let them go. What's happening here is pretty nasty isn't it? You don't want to be part of it. Tell them they can go through.'

Lev looked round for the boy with the knarled hands.

'New York?'

The young soldier looked surprised.

'Yes. I am. How did you know?'

'Accent, and you look like a New Yorker.'

'I do?'

'Yes, very. Let them be, these people. This is not right, what's happening here, you must realise that?'

He heard the girl soldier snigger behind him. Lev turned round to face her. He attempted to catch her eye, but they were hard and unflinching.

'What's your game?' she demanded. 'Why are you doing this? I want your passport back. I want to find out exactly who you are.'

'My name is Lev Dubnow and I'm a Jew just like you.'

She scoffed.

'Really?! I think you'd better come with us.'

'No.'

'What was that? What did you say?'

'I said no.'

'Do what I tell you.'

'I promise I'll come with you if you start letting these people through. They've waited long enough.'

'They can wait.'

'They can't. Let them through.'

'They can wait I tell you. Dan, bring him.'

The boy from New York tried to take Lev's arm but Lev shook himself free.

'Leave me alone, Dan.'

He turned back to the girl.

'Let these people through and I'll come with you gladly.'

'I've told you my decision. I've told you to come with us and you will.'

'What are you going to do young lady, get Dan and his mate to drag me away by my hair?'

'If necessary.'

'Then do it. Go on, do it.'

The watching crowd had slowly and silently shifted forward. The three soldiers suddenly realised how close they had come to them. Dan was the first to react, and he flared. Using the butt of his rifle as he had done before, and kicking at the dusty earth, he turned on them wildly.

'Get back! Get back, do you hear?'

This time though, those at the front, including Omar, stood their ground.

'Get back! I order you to get back!'

Lev jumped in front of Dan, between him and what seemed suddenly a solid mass of people, inexorably moving forward.

'Dan, stop that. Let them go through. Can't you see? You

can't stop them now. Finish this before someone gets hurt. Stand aside.'

'It's you who have done this.'

'Don't talk rubbish Dan.'

A murmur went through the crowd. 'Soldiers. Soldiers. The soldiers.'

Lev looked back at them.

For the first time since arriving in Israel, Lev heard the sharp, alien cracks of gunfire. The sound gave Dan courage.

'Call yourself a Jew.'

Lev felt the heavy thud of Dan's rifle butt on the back of his head, his chin jerked sharply forward on to his chest and he lost his footing. Pain filled his head in one single intense throb. His skull felt as if it was going to burst. He was on the ground, his mouth was full of dust, feet were stamping and scuffing the earth all around him and he couldn't see clearly anymore.

'It's your fault this has happened.' It was the tiny girl soldier. He recognised her tough, unyielding little voice. 'Call yourself a Jew.'

He felt her kicking at his body. He buried his head in his arms, screwed himself up tight, his knees against his chest. He began to lose consciousness.

A voice through a loudspeaker warned that shots would be fired into the crowd if it didn't retreat. The crowd obeyed and withdrew to behind the concrete blocks. The three soldiers had also backed off. Together with reinforcements from the military camp up on the hill, they stood behind the pillbox, from which the barrel of a large field piece ranged across the terrified crowd.

Lev's twisted body was left alone, a motionless, crumpled

heap in the centre of the now cleared ground. Scattered around it, some crushed underfoot, were the white bars of soap Lev had bought in Nablus just an hour before. The black plastic bag had split and they had tumbled out on to the ground as he fell. Bright fresh blood trickled from the back of his head.

\* \* \*

That evening, an image was shown on the news bulletins of most European television stations: Lev's huddled, lonely body, surrounded by what looked like smashed tablets of white stone. The same shot appeared again the next day on the front pages of most morning newspapers.

The following Wednesday, a documentary was broadcast on German television, called *Young Jews Say 'Enough!'*. A short sequence, slotted in at the last minute, was introduced by the reporter as 'a shocking incident, filmed last week at Nablus Checkpoint.'

# Afterwards

'Blood was bubbling in my mouth, Jo. I could feel it. It was hot and cloying, clinging to the roof of my mouth, covering my lips. I had to sit up. I knew I had to sit up. I knew I would die there in Sarah's hallway if I didn't. I spat some blood out and thankfully whoever was holding me down sprang back to avoid it and because of that, and only because of that, I managed to prop myself against the wall. I was gasping. I spat more blood out of my mouth. It was warm. I felt myself being lifted on to a trolley bed. It was the ambulance people. And they tried to force me to lie down as well. They even tried to strap me down. "Just you rest quiet sir, while we get you into the back of the ambulance. We know what we're doing; you're in good hands now." I can tell you it took quite an effort, but I said in as steady a voice as I could manage, "Listen to me. I'm a doctor. I'm a doctor. Do you understand me? If you lay me down, I will die, I will die. Do you hear me? If you don't do what I say, I will die. You do have oxygen? You do have the right equipment?" One of the crew nodded. I could see bewilderment in his eyes, he was fazed with panic. But I knew I wasn't about to die, Jo, I knew.'

'I don't see how you could have been so certain.'

'Everything in my experience as a doctor has told me

that death is never instantaneous. It's a process. The chill comes first. I've often seen what looks like a brief wince cross the face when it's first felt. After it has worked its way through the body it gently fades away. It must feel very strange when hot and cold cease to be sensations. When that time comes, when the coldness has gone, the dying know that there's no hope left; that's when death is faced, when the dying finally see life for what it really is.'

'And that is?'

'A detail.'

'A detail?'

'I can't think of a better word. In the end very few people "rage against the dying of the light", Jo, very few.'

'I can't remember you talking like this before.'

'Can't you? Do you think I may finally be thinking for myself rather than second-hand through you? Isn't that what you've always wanted?'

She reached out and lightly touched his wrist. 'I suppose I have, although I have to say I find your conclusions profoundly depressing.'

'You do? Why? I find them profoundly consoling. Whatever our experience of life, good or bad, happy or sad, however painful or easeful the death, the final experience for us all is the same. It is peaceful, embraced gladly and without a backward look.'

Joanna was silent. Her broad forehead, criss-crossed with faint, taut lines, betrayed her puzzled surprise.

'If life's a mere detail, where does that leave what we choose to do with our lives?'

'Unimportant details too, I'm afraid.'

'Is all this a consequence of your visit to Israel?'

'Mostly, but these things are cumulative aren't they? A couple of decades in Accident and Emergency have something to do with it. I've watched so many different sorts of people die in so many different ways, and at such close quarters. But yes certainly, witnessing at first hand, as I have just done, how badly people are behaving in Israel and Palestine has made a very deep impression on me. It's a land crammed with the remnants of so many lost and forgotten peoples, now no more than footnotes in history.'

'If what we do is all so unimportant, what was the 'Nablus Incident' all about? Why did you bother to get yourself involved?'

'Must have temporarily lost the plot. Dazzled by Rachel Sahed?'

He grinned at her.

'Good-looking woman is she?'

'Not especially, but I have always been susceptible to a pretty face, haven't I?'

'And us? You left Israel, your family, and your home because of 'us', remember?' Why did you bother?'

'*It must have been you who dazzled me that time.*' Lev laughed. 'You did, you know.'

'What?'

'Dazzle me.'

Now Joanna surprised him.

'You've been very brave, Lev, very brave indeed. You shouldn't make light of what you did, on both occasions. At Nablus you could have died.'

'Would that have been so terrible? And who knows? My death might have had a positive effect on how things are there.'

'From the little you've told me, isn't that rather optimistic? At best you would have been a news item for a couple of days. A footnote in history. A detail.'

\* \* \*

'You've been very fortunate, Dr Dubnow. You are all patched up now but you were very lucky, very lucky indeed. You could have died.'

Looking down on him, as he awoke, was a young female doctor with the newly discovered joy of saving a life shining in her eyes.

Lev was lying in a hospital bed. Everything around him was clean, white and bright.

'If it hadn't been for the ambulance crew doing exactly the right thing you would have died in the back of their ambulance.'

'Thank them for me, will you?'

'I certainly shall. Mind you, your assailant was a bit of an amateur. He only managed to put a little hole in the bottom of one of your lungs. Lucky for you he had such poor aim.'

'He was very agitated.'

'He was one of those fanatics, that's what he was. From one of those settlements up near the Syrian border, I shouldn't wonder.'

Lev looked up at her and knew what she wanted to hear him say, like all young doctors.

'And thank you, doctor, for what you and your colleagues have done for me. I am sitting here now because of what you all did for me and I am very grateful.'

She nodded in acknowledgement, happy that she had played a part in his survival.

'You have become very famous, Dr Dubnow. There are dozens of reporters outside. We've been forbidden to talk to them about you and had instructions not to let them near your room. They've even sent security to guard your corridor.'

'Is that right? I'm not likely to get stabbed again then?'

'Very unlikely I should say. It is all very exciting!'

The young doctor giggled.

Her boss was a lot sterner. A short, untidy man, the pockets of his grubby white coat were overflowing with crumpled papers curling at the edges, his thin grey hair unkempt. Even his black yarmulke was stained. His eyes were small and penetrating – fever-bright but completely humourless.

'We treat our patients, Dr Dubnow, and save their lives, if we can, whatever we think of them.'

'I'm sure you do.'

'I expect you know why that young man stabbed you?'

'I have an idea.'

'I'm sure you have. And while I don't agree with what he did, I agree absolutely with why he did it. You should have been thrown out of the country immediately after your pathetic little escapade at Nablus. I can't think why the authorities allowed you to stay after what you did. Now that young man has attacked you, you've become even more of a sensation for the newspapers all over the world to write about.'

'If you want to call what I did at Nablus pathetic I have no problem with that. What I do have a problem with is what has happened to me as a result. The man who stabbed me was a complete stranger, who knew nothing about me except what he had read in the newspapers. And now it is my doctor who thinks he is justified in haranguing me. Apart from anything else, Doctor, since I'm in one of your beds, in one of your wards, in your hospital, your professional conduct is questionable, to say the least.'

'Fine words, Dr Dubnow; fine, indignant, self-righteous words, which I don't really want to stand here and listen to. I suggest you leave Israel as soon as you are recovered, which I expect will be quite soon. You are healing very rapidly.'

'I don't have to go anywhere. I am a Jew and I have a right to be here.'

'I understand you now have a British passport and live and practise in London.'

'Whatever my present nationality, I'm still a Jew. And what is more I'm a Jew in Israel. While I am here, Doctor, I claim the right to express what I feel about what is happening here and to criticise, however crudely some may think I do it.'

'You clearly see yourself as very important. You don't behave like a Jew, Dr Dubnow. No one wants you here. Your very presence in Israel has helped to undermine us, and what we, who live here, are trying to do.'

'And what is that, in your view?'

'That a son of Levi Dubnow should ask such a question! Exist, Dr Dubnow, exist. Make lives for ourselves and our children. Make this land bloom, where once it lay wasted and unused. Not to give in to those who seek to destroy us – three times we have repelled our Arab enemies in little more than fifty years, and will three times more, in the next fifty, if necessary. We will not be humiliated yet again. We will eradicate, through determined resistance and courage, the memory of what the world has done to us for thousands of years. We will fight, whatever the cost, against anyone who questions our right to be here.'

\* \* \*

Three days later, Lev was taken back to Sarah's flat under cover of darkness, through the morgue tunnel. He was told to take it easy for a few more days, but he did not need to be told. He had been discharged too early. Sarah worried and fretted. She had not been allowed to visit him while he had been in hospital, nor had he been allowed to make or receive phone calls. Her only news of his progress was from the television and newspapers.

As soon as he had a private moment, he rang Joanna to tell her he was OK. She had rung Sarah already but Sarah had been able to tell her only that he was alive, and apparently on the mend. She was relieved, she said, to hear his voice sounding so strong, and told him to call her as soon as he returned to England.

Three weeks later, the press who had been camped outside had all but gone. There had also been a couple of guards posted in the apartment building, primarily to keep the reporters out but probably also to keep Lev in. He had not attempted to leave because he had not felt well enough, but he was sure they would not have let him if he had tried. He had suffered from a slight fever for a few days, which he had weathered, and his back wound seemed to have healed well, although he still had a little discomfort when he breathed deeply. He supposed there must be some tender scar tissue in there somewhere. Sarah wanted to call the consultant but Lev persuaded her it wasn't necessary.

Although his minders seemed less in evidence now, he still felt he was being closely watched. He thought he might have heard from Rachel but had not.

Lev was sitting reading in Sarah's living room when Udi turned up. It was the first time Lev had seen or spoken to him since they had met in the Begin Salon. Udi had let himself in with his own key, knowing that Sarah would be out for the morning. Lev thought that perhaps they had prearranged things.

'Hi. You feeling better?'

'Not so bad. There's not much pain anymore but I still get very tired if I move about too much.' Lev grinned. 'So I don't, as you can see. You know where Sarah's kitchen is, don't you? If you want a drink.'

'Thanks. I'm fine. Sarah said you've not made any move to return home yet.'

'No I haven't. Arrangements for returning to London haven't been the foremost thing on my mind. I wouldn't have made any without seeing you first.'

'You wouldn't?'

'No. Of course not. I've been worried that events might overtake me before we saw each other. Since Nablus quite a lot of unexpected things have happened. I'm very glad you've come by.'

Udi failed to react to Lev's reference to 'the incident' – deliberately or otherwise Lev couldn't judge, so blank was his brother's expression.

'Sarah thought you might be thinking of staying on.'

'What, for good? A bit of wishful thinking. Dear Sarah. I'm touched. No, Udi, I couldn't live in Israel. And anyway I'm not wanted here am I? Although I'll admit it will be very

hard to leave. It will almost seem like I'm deserting again.'
Lev grinned but Udi remained impassive. 'If I did stay, Udi,
I'd have to be active in some sort of meaningful way.'

'You would?'

'How else could I justify living here? It would be like
endorsing what's happening and I couldn't bring myself to
do that.'

'I see.'

Udi sat down on the sofa.

'It's a mess here though, Udi, isn't it?'

'It is not ideal, I grant you.'

'Not ideal! It could turn very easily into a disaster of epic
proportions.'

'Some might think that is slightly exaggerating the situation.'

'And they'd be wrong, Udi. In a world where a nuclear
device of some sort can be purchased for the price of a flat
in central London anything could happen here at any time.
Israel's behaviour at the moment is so wretched that it is
almost provoking the Palestinians into an extreme response.
Corner a rat and it'll go for your throat. From what I've seen,
people on the West Bank are in that corner already. They are
being killed daily, publicly humiliated at every checkpoint,
their homes are being destroyed indiscriminately and their
freedom curtailed to such a degree that they can barely
make a living, and in a lot of cases they aren't even managing to do that. Now, like at no other time in its history, Israel
is betraying the beliefs and principles that brought us Jews
here in the first place, scripture is being defied and distorted
for entirely political ends or not even being referred to at all,
and secular politicians have been chosen to lead who barely

bother to shelter under the cope of Judaism anymore. Most of today's Israelis have forgotten why it's so important that we are here in Palestine. They have resigned themselves to the inevitability of the violence and killing.'

Udi remained impassive as Lev continued.

'Our parents fear for their children's safety going to school and we then threaten the daily lives of Arab parents so that they fear for their children too. Have you been to Hebron? Would you really rather have Arab men and boys disconsolately sipping tea and playing cards in its deserted Old City and in refugee camps and deserted villages elsewhere, than working, making things, selling things, decently providing for their families? Would you rather slowly destroy Nablus, crush one by one its thousand-year-old buildings and with them the spirit of its people, than restore and refurbish it? We foster disrespect rather than respect; we humiliate old Palestinian men rather than revere them for their age and wisdom; we try and ignore, or worse, abuse and ridicule, rather than befriend. It is time to tell ourselves we've won. That we have done enough. That our enemy is tired, abject, on its knees. Now is the time to be generous. They've had it Udi; they'll take peace at almost any price.

'I haven't the words to express to you the pain and distress I have felt when I've witnessed the daily, almost casual, cruelty being meted out here. Meted out by my people Udi. That's what's so hard. They are my people who are behaving so badly. People I am supposed to understand, know and love. People who were brought up, nurtured and educated like me. No one now can ever tell me that it's not really as bad as all that because I, me, this person here in front of you, has witnessed it. Witnessed it with my own eyes.

'I don't regret what I did at Nablus, however pathetic and insignificant others may think it was, however unfair it was to the young soldiers who were caught up in it and who will probably get disciplined because of it. Neither do I regret that that young man stabbed me. '

Lev put his head back. He was tired. Somewhere deep in his body there was a dull ache. He felt an intense desire to curl up and sleep but there was still something he wanted to say. He made the effort and sat up straight again.

'You've been very quiet, Udi.'

Lev had hoped Udi would respond in some way, that there would be some sort of dialogue. But although Udi was clearly listening to his brother attentively, he remained expression-less and apparently unmoved. Lev doggedly pressed on.

'We may be brothers Udi but we're almost complete strangers, aren't we? Strangers who know each other very well. What is sad for me is that our knowledge of one another alienates us from each other rather than brings us closer together. I'm drawing a line under the past, big brother. I hope you'll be able to do that as well. You have nothing to fear from me, Udi, I mean you no harm. I only want the best for you.' Lev paused, looked hard at his brother, 'I'm glad to have had the opportunity to say what I've said. I wanted to say it to you, to you, my brother, whom I love.'

Lev sat back against the arm of the sofa and closed his eyes for a moment. He was out of breath. He had tears in his eyes.

'You do understand what I'm saying, don't you, Udi?'

'I do, yes.'

'Thanks for that much at least. It's all been worth it then. I'm tired now Udi. I need to rest. I hope you will come to

London and visit me sometime and that it'll be a good deal better between us then than it has been this time. I'll let you know when I've made the flight arrangements, so hopefully we'll get a chance to see each other before I leave. Go now Udi, please. You'll let yourself out? Love to Leah.'

'Bye, Lev. See you in London, if I don't see you before.'

'Bye, Udi.'

✻ ✻ ✻

*It was bright sun before. I liked that. I like the sun. High and bright and warm on my back. In here I can't see it. It's gone. Here the streets are too crowded, too dark. I can't see my way there's so many people. It's like I'm in a forest of moving trees. Shouting, yelling above my head. Legs, skirts and shoes. Slippers decorated with frayed gold brocade. So many shoes. Shoes everywhere. All I can see are legs, skirts and shoes. Where's Dad, where's Udi? They were there a minute ago. Where are they now? Left then right. Or is it right then left? I can't remember. I can't ask. Can I ask? I can't. I won't be understood.*

*'I don't think you know where you are little master. I think you're lost. Are you lost? Give me your hand, young man, and we'll see if we can find your father. I think I know where you are supposed to be.'*

*How can he know where Dad and Udi are? He's so big. But he speaks just like me. I can understand what he's saying. They don't understand us, Dad said. They'll never understand us. They don't want to understand us. His hand is so soft, just like Dad's. His voice is so low! And he doesn't smell. Dad said they smell. Why did he tell me that? He doesn't. He's so gentle. The whites of his eyes are so red. They're like fire.*

*'Please. Where are we going? Where are you taking me?'*

*'Found your tongue little man have you? Don't be frightened. I'm taking you to your father. I know where he'll be. It's Shabbat. A good Jew will only be in one place on Shabbat and your father's a good Jew, I'm sure. Let's turn down this little street. This one here. There. Now you know where you are don't you?'*

*I know where we are. We're here. This is the square, there's the Wall.*

*'Yes. I know this place. I know where I am.'*

*'We must stand where we are, we must look for your father from here, I'm afraid. I can't go any further. I wouldn't be welcome. Not there. Can you see your father? Can you see him anywhere?'*

*'Lev where have you been?'*

*'Let him out of your sight for a moment and he gets himself lost, Dad. We should have left him at home. He's always such a nuisance.'*

*'Where's he gone? Where's the Arab man gone?'*

*'You could have got lost Lev. Thanks be to God you found your way.'*

*'But I didn't. That man, that tall Arab man found my way for me. Where's he gone?'*

*'What was that you were saying, Lev?'*

Lev awoke with a start. Udi had let himself out.

\* \* \*

The following Sunday morning just before dawn the doorbell rang. Lev heard Sarah get up and rattle through the bead curtain as she went out into the hall.

'Who is it?' she asked.

There was suspicion and alarm in her voice. Lev heard a muffled response; he could imagine her peering through the spy hole. He then heard her unhooking the chain, pulling the bolts and opening the front door. She came back through to him.

'Lev, are you awake? There is someone to see you.'

A tall man came into the room, dressed casually, an identity card dangling from his neck. Lev lifted his head from the pillow and propped himself up on his elbow. He pointedly ignored his visitor and spoke directly to his sister.

'I'm sorry; I still haven't bought you the new dressing gown I promised you.'

'That doesn't matter, Lev. We can go today, if you like. If you have time.'

'I think my time has just run out Sarah.'

Sarah looked uneasily between the two men.

'Shall I get us all some coffee?'

'Thank you, that's very kind but no. I don't want to hurry you unduly, Dr Dubnow, but since we were talking about time, it is something we are running a little short of.'

Lev put on his new spectacles and finally looked up at the newcomer.

'You can say that again!'

'I beg your pardon, Dr Dubnow?'

Lev disregarded his question and asked a question of his own – one to which he already knew the answer.

'You've come to deport me, I suppose?'

'I have, Dr Dubnow. There is a car and driver downstairs waiting to take us to Ben Gurion.'

'Does it have to be Ben Gurion?'

'It does, yes.'

'Does that mean my passport will get stamped?'

'Not if you don't want us to, sir.'

'Thanks. Thanks very much.'

In response, the tall official smiled, gently inclining his head down and to one side, putting his right hand flat on his chest, his fingers splayed.

'I'll need to pack a suitcase.'

'Naturally.'